Youngsters

Craig McCabe

Published by Trend February 2008

Copyright Craig McCabe

Craig McCabe has asserted his right under the Copyright, Designs and Parents Act 1988 to be identified as the author of this work.

ISBN 9780955741715

Acknowledgements

Thanks to all my family and friends for all their continued support, (maybe now you'll take me serious about all this writing nonsense), thanks to Ryan for making my idea for the cover a reality, Big Jim, Billy, Sambo, Dej and not forgetting Ginger Liam.

A special thanks goes to Helen for helping me out at such short notice and to all the people who read my first novel and passed on their words of encourage.

www.craigmcabe.co.uk

1.

Adam was only four when his parents were killed. They were driving home during a bad winter when a lorry lost control due to black ice and hit them head on killing them instantly. Adam never had any other family to take care of him except an older brother Billy. Billy had constantly led a life of crime since he was a teenager and was becoming more and more of a handful for the police as he got older. His life of crime was beginning to catch up with him and he was also struggling to cope with this tragedy in his life. He wanted to take care of Adam and become his legal guardian but due to his age and the constant trouble he was finding himself in he knew it would only be a matter of time before they took him away.

  He approached old Charlie and his wife Kathy who were friends of his parents and asked if they would foster Adam. They had never had any children of their own and Billy knew they would give Adam anything he needed. They lived in a large house surrounded by fields on the outskirts of Dundee. Billy would come to visit Adam occasionally and Charlie would always try and persuade him to stay. Charlie knew what was going on. He knew how much trouble Billy was in and that he was about to be locked up for a long spell. The last time Adam saw Billy was when he turned up at old Charlie's late one night with a holdall full of his belongings. Adam remembers Billy giving him a hug and saying that he was going away for a while and he would be in touch as often as he could. It was around this time the police came by, several times, looking for Billy and each time Charlie would get more aggressive before shutting the door on them. A while later Adam received a letter from Billy that had been stamped in a country that he couldn't even pronounce. This went on for many years, as each letter he received would be posted from a different country. Adam loved reading about Billy's adventures and every once in a while Billy would stay long enough in the same place for Adam to write back. At school Adam found it hard to bond with the other children as he was far superior both physically and mentally for his age. Adam had learned so much about life from old Charlie who was always willing to pass on his knowledge and advice.

Adam lived with Charlie and Kathy for six years until, not long after his tenth birthday, old Charlie had a heart attack and died. This was the moment when his whole life caved in for a second time. The authorities in all their worldly wisdom had decided that Kathy, due to her age wasn't capable of looking after a ten year old boy on her own and decided to move him on to another foster home.

Within days of moving in with his new foster parents he had learned with a harsh reality, nothing was ever going to be the same again. The loving, caring, secure environment he had grown to appreciate disappeared with a slap across the face as punishment for leaving his school bag lying on the floor in the hallway. Adam didn't cry like most ten year old boys would do when a fifteen stone grown man floored them. He didn't even make a sound. He stood up, put his hand to his swollen face and in silence stared back in total shock and anger. Although old Charlie had taught him many ways to defend himself, and for a ten year old boy who had been involved in many fights at school, he was more than capable of taking punches from other boys that were two, sometimes three years his senior, he knew he had no chance against a grown man who was twice his size and weight.

That first slap was the start of a two year struggle against physical abuse that he had to endure from Harry, his new foster father. There was never any verbal abuse from Harry, that all came from Linda his new foster mother. Each time he heard her ranting and raving at Harry he knew what was coming. How this deranged couple could ever have past the governments so called strict vetting policy was shocking. It wasn't long after that first slap that the beatings really started. Adam would try his best to fight back but each time he stood up to Harry the beatings got more severe. Harry wasn't stupid though, he hardly ever hit Adam where it would show. The back of the head was his favourite and sometimes when Adam stood his ground, the stick would come out, but this was only used on Adam's legs, the lower the better as these would be explained as football injuries.

During these two years Adam ran away several times. He had a social worker assigned to his case and Adam told him on many occasions that he was being abused and had actually shown the bruises that he endured from one of his beatings from Harry. This was all to no avail as Harry quickly dismissed them as bruises from Adam fighting at school. It was also during this time that Adam lost contact with Billy. He still sent letters and Kathy reposted them to Adam's new address but he never received them. Every time Adam ran away he made his way to Kathy's house but the police knew where he was heading and would be sitting waiting on him when he arrived.

Two years later Kathy had to move into a residential home due to her age and Adam was never informed. He ran away once again and was found sitting on the door step of the boarded up home. He was returned once more to his foster parents home where, as usual they would create a whiter than white environment for the benefit of the social workers and police. He was told for his own benefit and for Kathy's health that he would not be given her new address. As soon as they left and their cars were driven down the street out of sight, Adam knew what was coming. He was shaking with fear and anger as Harry sat opposite him with his evil stare waiting on Linda to finish her tirade of abuse. She went on and on at how they took him in when he had no-one and this was how he repaid them by bringing the police to her door. It was time for Harry to teach him a lesson he would never forget. Adam was sent to his room. He sat on the edge of his bed and tried to prepare himself mentally for what was about to come. He could hear them downstairs arguing and then the sound of heavy footsteps. He couldn't take it any longer. Knowing now that he didn't even have anywhere to run away to, he decided he had had enough. The bedroom door opened and Harry stood as he had done previously, only this time he had his belt wrapped around his knuckles with the buckle hanging down past his large gut. Adam stood up, legs like jelly, and gritted his teeth. Harry walked towards him with sheer anger in his eyes and raised his arm up behind him. In the split second it took for Harry to swing the belt down Adam kicked him in the shin with everything he had. It wasn't enough to stop the momentum of the swing. The belt hit Adam on the top of his head sending him to the floor. He looked up clutching his head and saw Harry raising his arm once more.

"I'm going to teach you a real lesson this time" Harry says with total rage in his eyes.

Adam leaned forward and grabbed Harry's leg with both hands, opening his mouth as wide as he could he sank his teeth in and bit him. Harry let out a loud howl and dropped both hands to clutch his leg. Adam got to his feet and with Harry crouching down they were now at face level. Adam, who had been taught by old Charlie to defend himself when he had been bullied in the playground, had also learned many moves that were not for the playground. The type of actions to use only when he had to... now was one of those times. Without a second thought Adam raised two fingers and in a fast, powerful, stabbing motion he poked Harry in the eyes. Harry howled again and stood upright. He staggered around the room with his hands covering his face shouting that he couldn't see. Adam looked at the clear doorway and made a run for it. As he attempted to sneak past Harry he grabbed a hold of him. They struggled and fell to the floor and Adam tried to scramble away as he fought him off. He had a hold of Adam with one hand and was punching him with the other. Adam looked up and saw a lamp that had been smashed in the struggle. He picked up a sharp piece of porcelain and as Harry couldn't see he lifted it above him and stabbed Harry in the back. He released Adam and cried out in agony shouting for Linda. Adam ran out of the room and barged past Linda who was making her way up the stairs. He ran out of the house and down the street in the direction of Kathy's and kept on running until he was out of breath and he could not run anymore. He sat down by the side of the road waiting for his breathing to return to normal. The tears start to roll down his cheeks. He hadn't cried in a long, long time. Not even after a hard beating from Harry. He sat for a while thinking about Kathy and why she would move away without telling him. He felt lost and had nowhere to turn to.

Wiping the tears from his face as he stood, he walked back to his foster parent's house just in time to see Harry being put in the ambulance. A neighbour pointed Adam out to the police who were busy questioning Linda, they came over and Adam was escorted into the back of the patrol car.

Due to the severity of the assault on his foster father Adam was placed into a secure children's home. The secure home was generally used to accommodate young offenders aged twelve to fourteen and was run by the local authority social services department. It was a home to some of the most vulnerable young teenagers in the area and although it had a bad reputation, it didn't faze Adam in the slightest as anything was better than having to face Harry and Linda again. Adam was the youngest in the home by a few months and the most susceptible to being bullied. All the boys in the home had come from tough backgrounds where most had been abused to some extent. There was the usual power struggle amongst them that you would find in almost any school playground. And the staff would turn a blind eye to most of it. Adam kept to himself but he knew it was only a matter of time before the other boys started to show their authority. Since he arrived he had watched them push some of the other boys around and take their allowance money from them. One of the boys had made the mistake of grassing and found himself with a severe beating. Adam was on his own when two of the older boys confronted him. He was cornered in the toilet one day and the two bullies started on him without saying a word. Adam fought back. The punches and kicks the boys threw at him were nothing to what he had received from Harry. Adam walked out of the toilet first and left the two bullies in a mess on the floor. As far as Adam was concerned that was the end of the matter but no, this drew the attention of older, harder boys that now saw Adam as a threat. The more Adam was taunted and bullied the more he fought back. Before long Adam had a reputation as one who was not to be messed with. Although this brought its own trouble as there would always be someone who wanted to relieve Adam of this reputation, no one more so than the staff themselves. They had taken a dislike to Adam due to the influence he was having over the other boys. Every new boy who came to the secure home brought with them a bigger swagger and a larger chip on their shoulder. It was only a matter of time before they tried it on. The staff didn't help the situation as they constantly wound the boys up at every opportunity. These were grown men who took pleasure in bullying and beating up vulnerable young boys that they were supposed to be helping. When a fight broke out between two of the boys this gave the staff the opportunity to use force. Adam dealt with it in his usual way, by inflicting as much damage as possible. Each incident that Adam was involved in was noted on his record and resulted in the authorities finding it more difficult to place him in a new foster home. Adam didn't mind until he was informed that when he reached the age of fifteen he would be transferred to a Young Offenders Institution. This was a facility run by the prison service and accommodated fifteen to twenty-one year olds. The way the other boys talked, the secure home was like a holiday camp compared to the institution. This information had a major effect on Adam as he started to avoid the staff as much as possible and managed to stay out of trouble for a long time. Due to his sudden change in behaviour Adam's social worker had allocated him the next available foster home. This could not come quickly enough for him as a new 'hard case' had been brought into the unit. His name was Bryn and Adam knew as soon as the boy walked through the door there would be trouble. He was tall for his age and quite skinny but he had a hard rough look about him for a boy of only fourteen. It was only his first day and he was making demands on some of the younger boys in the unit. Some of the boys approached Adam and asked when he was going to sort him out. Adam wasn't going looking for it, he knew it would happen, it was just a matter of how and when. The staff were constantly on his case telling him that he had lost his bottle. Adam went about his business as he had always done. In a little under a week of Bryn arriving their paths eventually crossed. The staff knew what was about to happen and made themselves scarce. Adam was lying on his bed when his door swung open.

"I hear you're the top man around here"

As Adam went to get up Bryn lunged forward with a fist. It caught Adam on the side of the face and he felt the sting immediately. Another fist came at him but Adam managed to get out of the way and throw one of his own. The two boys traded punches until both boys fell back onto the bed. Adam was on top and grabbed Bryn by the hair and smashed the back of his head on the bed post. Adam stood up as Bryn rolled onto the floor clutching the back of his head with both hands. Adam was about to walk out of the room when he felt a sharp pain in the back of his calf. He turned to see Bryn with a blade in his hand. He crouched down to clutch his leg and saw the blood soaking through his trousers. He swung the blade again but Adam stepped back. Bryn got to his feet and charged at Adam. Using both his hands Adam grabbed the wrist holding the blade. The two boys wrestled to the floor and the blade was dropped. Other boys had heard the commotion and alerted the staff, who took their time in attending the scene. As they arrived

Adam was on top of Bryn throwing punch after punch to his head. He was dragged off by two members of staff and taken to hospital. As he lay in the bed with his leg stitched up Adam had a visit from his social worker. He was given some good news that he had been waiting for. In light of the latest incident the authorities had decided that he would not be placed in a new foster home, although bad news was to follow. Due to the severity of the incident, and the fabricated reports from the staff, Adam would not be allowed to return to the secure home and instead would be transferred temporarily to a Young Offenders Institution. Adam pleaded his case saying that Bryn had come for him and that he had also produced the blade. But this was all to no avail as his social worker was part of the system and therefore backed the staff's report that Adam was difficult and hard to control. Although Borstal had officially been closed since 1982 the Y.O.I. to boys like Adam was still known as Borstal.

2.

A new project was in the process of being set up, which started the year previous to Adam being sent to the Y.O.I., involving an active social worker named Jason Fallon, Jay to most people who knew him. He had thought of the program several years before and had gradually worked to gain the interest and backing from the appropriate authorities. The project was titled 'The Program' and consisted of a home to cater for no more than ten selected candidates. Including Jay, there would be three full time staff. This was not a place where the worst offenders could go as a cop out from being detained in an institution. The Program would be set in a relaxed environment were a chosen few would be trusted to abide by the rules. Jay had grown up with the same background of abuse, violence and crime as with most of the kids that he worked with. It was during a spell in prison that he decided to put his life on the straight and narrow and began to study. After his release he worked as a volunteer advising troubled teenagers who appeared to be going down the same path, making the wrong choices he had. Jay was eventually awarded with a permanent position. Over the years he had worked with some of the worst cases any social worker could come across. Through his help and advice, some of these teenagers had managed to turn their lives around, although this was not an overnight transition.

Jay worked with them in all aspects of their life by helping them change their whole attitude and outlook towards other people and themselves.

Before the boys were selected for the program Jay would study the files and backgrounds of boys that had a possibility of reforming. He would work with them to create an environment where they would be under no pressure from outside influences but if they broke the rules they would not be given a second chance and would be sent straight back to where they came from.

Over the years Jay had received awards and praise for his work and dedication in helping these vulnerable teenagers. When the decision came to award the funding for his program all the Board members had agreed, all accept one. The only objection came from Councillor Williamson. This was a vicious ruthless beast of a man who ran the council with an iron fist. He had gone on record to say that he thought The Program was a waste of public money and that it was destined to fail. Putting all these violent teenagers in one place to roam free and cater for themselves was in no way going to change them into becoming caring law abiding decent citizens. Councillor Williamson had an ulterior motive to his objection. He had a history with Jay and did not like the fact that he had once been a criminal himself and was now considered a respected member of society. The funds that were set aside for The Project had been promised to Williamson only several months previously for one of his own useless promotional projects. After many meetings and long discussions the Board had decided to fund The Program for two years. The turning point for the Board was that if the program was successful after the first two years a local businessman would fund it for the next three. Williamson now had an axe to grind with the other Board members as they voted in favour of Jay's project.

Accommodation for The Program was a purpose built unit on the outskirts of Dundee. The building was set in a large area surrounded by fields and had two separate dorms for the boys which were set out in an army style barracks. A class room, a large lounge, three separate supervisors rooms, a kitchen with dining area, toilets, shower rooms and an office. A small mini bus was also allocated for the program. Although Jay would be the head supervisor there would be two full time wardens and one part time warden apparently employed for security reasons only. These were at the recommendation of Councillor Williamson and they would be employed by his department. He insisted this was for Jay and the boys' safety, but everyone involved knew their job priority was to report back to Williamson. The Councillor would never give the project a chance and insisted on random visits and reports each week from the security wardens. After six months things were running smoothly. There were constant complaints by the boys about Frank and Bruce the two full time wardens who were bullying them when Jay was not around. As they were not employed by The Program Jay had no authority over these wardens and they had no say in how he ran it. But each time there was a complaint by one of the boys Jay had recorded it and logged the name, date time and details in a note book. The six monthly review was due and Jay was intending on producing these notes at the Board meeting.

Jay was constantly being handed files of boys that were being detained in a Y.O.I. or were about to be detained. After reading their past crimes and background checks more than half were handed back without a second look. These were boys who were destined for a life of crime with or without his help. Only real time in prison would make or break them.

The next boy who was about to leave The Program was Richard. Rich, as he was known, had turned sixteen and was now allowed to leave. He had been in the Young Offenders Institution for over a year when Jay picked him for the program. He had showed potential while in the institution and Jay requested he spend his last six months on the program. As Rich was the oldest of the other boys, Jay had made him the group leader and used him to relate to the other boys. This had proved successful, as he had befriended one of the more difficult cases. With Rich now leaving another boy was carefully chosen. Jay had his regular weekly meeting where he discussed the progress of the other boys and also passed on the file of the next candidate for the program. With his note book safely locked away with notes on the two security wardens he had still not found a member of the Board that he trusted to disclose the information to. He knew he had to tackle the problem soon before the wardens went too far and one of the boys kicked off and retaliated. This would suit Councillor Williamson as the whole program would be scrapped. Jay knew the Councillor was behind the warden's actions but he did not have proof and with all the other Board members afraid of him he had no choice but to hold on. Every time Jay enquired about the wardens he was immediately shot down from none other than Councillor Williamson. He always held back and let it go and would walk out of the meetings feeling stressed and disappointed that no-one else on the Board would back him. One day, while on his way to the lift, after another pointless meeting, one of the Board's representatives caught up with him. She was the only female on the Board and had a hardened attitude to her male colleagues. Upon entering the lift she handed over a folded piece of paper.

"What's this?" he says.

"It's a copy of a proposal that Blair put forward at the same time as your program"

"Who's Blair?"

"Councillor Williamson"

Jay smiled when it registered that the Councillor's first name was Blair.

"No wonder he insists on people calling him Councillor."

"You mentioned the security guys on your program."

"Yeah" Jay says.

"Look I can't say too much at the moment but I know everything that's happening on the program. Let's just say that I know it would be in Blair's best interest if The Program fails."

"Thanks for this" Jay says as the lift stops on ground level.

He goes to walk out and the turns and asks "Is there any particular reason that you are getting involved?"

"Yes but I can't tell you at the moment all I can say is that you are not alone on The Program"

Jay smiles as he walks off, but is confused to this new found ally.

When Williamson walked out of the meeting he felt close to an anxiety attack. He hated Jason Fallon and thought the ex criminal had no right to be in his presence whatsoever. The program wasn't meant to last two months but it had been running for six months with glowing reports and Jason Fallon was starting to ask questions about his wardens. He would have to step up the pressure. The Program had to fail and he had to get rid of Jason Fallon, whatever it would take.

3.

In the early Borstal days the wardens took it upon themselves to hand out severe physical punishments for petty rule breaking. When the Young Offenders Institution's were introduced the governors placed the responsibility onto the older boys to hand out the beatings. The Y.O.I. was intended for vulnerable boys aged between 15 to 21. Adam, having only recently turned 14 was informed that he was only being placed there until the authorities could find another secure home to accommodate him. The nearest Y.O.I. was situated on the west coast of Scotland and had a bad reputation. Adam was in the Institution for a little over a month and in that time he had been in front of the governor several times. At fourteen Adam was a well built lad but, along with his age and east coast accent, he was a target for bullies. Adam had no fear and treated people the same way they treated him. If someone was civil, he would be civil back. If someone tried it on no matter how old or what size they were, he met them head on. The boys who did try it on were the usual run of the mill bad boys. In those first two weeks Adam had proved to some of the older top boys that he was more than capable of handling himself. By the third week as he was to be informed about the program he had gained some new acquaintances who had taken him under his wing.

Jay had travelled down in the minibus and had taken Dylan, one of the other boys on The Program along with him. It was a couple of hours drive and having Dylan with him would maybe help Adam feel more at ease on the journey back to Dundee.

Adam was already in the reception area when Jay arrived. The governor had already informed him about The Program and the reasons he was chosen. After all the trouble Adam had been in since he arrived, the governor actually smiled at him, shook his hand and wished Adam good luck which was accompanied with advice about never returning in the future. Adam wondered if he gave the same speech to every person who left. Jay smiled and introduced himself while Adam, unsure of where or what he was moving onto, did not smile but lifted his head in acknowledgement. He picked up all his worldly possessions contained in his small holdall and the governor talked to Jay as he walked them back out to the minibus. Jay knew it was a good idea to bring Dylan along with him as he introduced himself to Adam and the two talked for most of the journey. Stopping only when their mouths were full of food as Jay stopped off for lunch on the way.

Dylan was fifteen, a year older than Adam but would pass for an eighteen year old. He was tall and stocky with large broad shoulders. He came across as a simple boy which resulted in other boys trying to take a loan of him. Dylan's parents were alcoholics and his childhood was spent taking beatings from his father on a regular basis. His mother was a wreck and she would also suffer at the hands of his father when Dylan wasn't around. Dylan would come home from school to see his mother with a black eye or a fat lip and this made him stop going to school. He wanted to be at home so that when his father felt the need to lash out, he would take the beating instead of his mother. The authorities were called every now and then and his father would get help. Things would be okay for a while but gradually it would end up back in the same routine. As Dylan got older the punches and kicks were not having the same effect as they used to, so the belt was introduced. At first, Dylan felt like he was being whipped. His body would sting for days afterwards. Sometimes the buckle would break through Dylan's skin and with blood seeping from his wounds his father would still continue his onslaught. All through these years of abuse Dylan hid the bruises and cuts. If someone happened to notice them he would make excuses and dream up bizarre stories to explain them. In his mind, if the authorities found out the truth he would have been taken into care, leaving his mother to receive the beatings. Through his years of continuous drunkenness his father had failed to notice that Dylan was growing. At fifteen he was six foot tall and now towered over his father.

At school, when he did turn up, he was nicknamed the gentle giant. The only time he got into trouble at school was for minor things like not doing his homework. He had a few friends but never anyone close enough that he could talk to. He did find himself a girlfriend, Sarah, and began to open up to her about the true extent of his home life. She was shocked when he revealed the extent of the marks on his body but he made her swear not to tell a soul. She did tell her parents who immediately phoned the authorities. This was not with the intention of helping Dylan. Sarah's father's sole purpose was in the hope of Dylan being taken into care and thus, stopping their daughter's relationship with him. Social services once again intervened but as always Dylan denied the marks were from abuse. After things settled, his father started on him again, for what would be the last time. Sarah was told not to see Dylan anymore by her father but they would secretly meet up.

One day while they skipped school and met up she knew something was bothering him, he was quieter than usual but he would not tell her what was on his mind. During the afternoon they spent together Dylan became more withdrawn as it came nearer time for them to return home. She knew it was something bad but she never asked. If Dylan wanted to tell her he would do it in his own time. He walked into his house and was greeted with his father's drunken rage after his two day bender. He continually cursed and blamed Sarah for all the trouble he had been through as Dylan crouched into his usual corner with his father standing over him striking him again and again with a wooden table leg, all the while shouting obscenities directed at Sarah. Dylan snapped. He stood up and faced his father. As he swung his arm to strike him once more Dylan pushed him. Due to his intoxication he stumbled back against the wall. Dylan grabbed the table leg and began hitting him repeatedly over the head. Dylan's mother came through screaming and tried to stop him. He turned around and looked at her with pure hatred and pushed her away in disgust and continued hitting his limp father all over his body. Due to his mothers screams a neighbour came running through and pulled Dylan away. He dropped the table leg, sat in a corner of the room and never said a word until the police and ambulance arrived. Dylan was arrested for attempted murder as his father was put in intensive care where he was kept on a life support machine for two weeks. He is now in a wheelchair and will need twenty four hour care for the rest of his life. After all the beatings he had handed out to his son throughout his whole childhood he still had the arrogance to have him charged. His mother did not speak up for him and stood by his father. Dylan was taken into care and was appointed a new social worker who requested that the charges be dropped to assault due to self defence. When the case was heard the father pushed for his son to go to trial for attempted murder and Dylan's mother was a witness.

Dylan's social worker put forward photos of the marks that the hospital found all over his body. The social worker fought the case hard and requested that Dylan not be sent to Borstal but to take part in a new program that was being set up. That social worker was Jay.

Jay had left the camp for a whole day and as usual he was worried when he had to leave his boys with the security wardens. But he had found a pattern to the bullying. It was only when Frank and Bruce were on a shift together that something happened. Today Jack was on. Jack was good with the boys, he was ex army and wasn't one for standing around. His job was to supervise but most of the time he got involved with whatever was going on. Jay thought he could do with a few more staff like that.

As he drove into the grounds of the camp the rest of the boys were outside kicking a ball around, but it appeared that some of them were more interested in kicking each other.

"Will I take Adam over to meet the rest of the boys Jay?" Dylan says as he climbs out of the minibus.

"No, Dylan you go and join them. I'm going to show Adam around the place and explain the rules of the program."

"Okay, I'll see you in a while Adam."

As Dylan walks over, two of the other boys are close to a punch up. Casey and Nazzir, or Naz as he prefers. Stuart, one of the other boys steps in between them to calm them down. Jay doesn't say anything as he is preoccupied with his new arrival, although he will have words with them later as it is becoming a daily occurrence seeing them niggling at each other to start a fight.

"More trouble come to join us Dylan?" Topher says as he

stands holding the ball waiting to get the game
started again.

"Hope it's not another Paki." Casey says as he tries to reach over and slap Naz again.

"I'm an Indian you ignorant racist pig."

"Oh I'm not a Paki, I'm an Indian." Casey says putting on a squeaky voice.

"Give it a break Casey. If Jay catches you saying that you'll be in big trouble man." Dylan says as he steps in to help split them up. He grabs a hold of Casey and drags him away.

"Get your hands off me you big dummy."
Dylan lets him go but stands in front of him and Casey puts on the hard man stance with his arms out wide squaring up to him. Dylan laughs at him and walks away.

"Yeah you had better walk away before I…"
Dylan turns back around and looks as though he is about to run at Casey, he takes a quick couple of steps and Casey runs off. Dylan turns back around to the other boys and they all laugh. He knows he wouldn't hit Casey and so do the other boys, only Casey doesn't know this.

Casey was one of the first boys to be considered for the program but this was not due to him committing any serious crime or that the authorities were about to lock him up. It was at his father's request. Casey's father was a very rich man and had a considerable amount of influence with the councillors on the Board. He had heard about The Program and at the time he was having extreme difficulty with his son. He knew the funding for the program was about to be rejected by one of his past business rivals, Williamson. Casey's father put forward a proposal that he would donate a considerable amount of money for the funding of the program if after the two year period it was successful. The only condition was that his son was placed on the program as he saw him becoming something of an embarrassment. Casey's father wanted Jay to give his son some direction in his life before he ended up in prison. Due to his proposal the Board was in favour of Jay's program. Since Casey was a young age he had always been the type of boy who sized people up and tried to prove he was the hardest and best fighter. He walked with the biggest swagger and talked and acted like 'a would be' hard man. He was constantly being thrown out of school or picked up by the police and most of the incidents related to assault. He latched on to a group of boys who went to watch football games. His father thought this was a good thing as he started taking an interest in his appearance and began wearing the latest designer clothes. It wasn't until he received a phone call that his son had been picked up and charged with racism and soccer violence that he realised his son was becoming a soccer casual.

Naz came from a large family; his parents came to Britain from India with five children excluding Naz. Although both his parents are Indian, Naz considers himself Scottish as this is the country he was born in. Most of Naz's family, who went to school in Dundee, had to endure the usual name calling and abuse just like many other Asian families. They handled it well by choosing to ignore it and walking away, but not Naz. He handled it in his own way, through violence. His parents were constantly being called up to his school due to him fighting with other pupils or arguing with teachers who he claimed were picking on him. He had switched schools so many times his parents were close to sending him over to India to live. Naz was a very intelligent boy and because of this his parents gave him chance after chance to stop turning to

violence. Naz was given counselling to help him deal with his problems and this worked for a short time until another disagreement with his maths teacher Mr. Kelly got out of hand. He was sent out of the class and the teacher followed. He closed the door behind him and slapped Naz hard across the back of the head.
Naz turned around and stood rooted to the spot in shock.

"Come on then. Where's your big mouth now?" The teacher said with his wide scary eyes. Naz couldn't speak, his mouth had gone dry and his chest felt tight. Mr. Kelly lifted his hand again and this time slapped Naz across the face. This sent him to the floor. Naz cowered away in fear. Mr Kelly stormed over and grabbed Naz by the neck lifting him up and pinning him against the wall. With his face only inches away from him Naz could smell his rotting breath when he said; "You're not so mouthy now are you? You little Paki bastard."

The grip around Naz's neck became tighter and he began to choke. Naz thought he was about to pass out when he heard the tip tap of a woman's heals coming along the corridor. It was Miss Ferrie, Naz's guidance teacher; he felt relieved that now he had a witness to him being assaulted. Mr Kelly released his grip slightly but still had him pinned to the wall.

"What's going on?" Miss Ferrie said.

"This little Paki has just lashed out at me."

"What? I never done anything. You sent me out of the class and hit me."

"Now Nazzir I don't think Mr. Kelly would hit you. Accusations like that could get you into a lot of trouble."

"But you've just heard him call me a Paki."

"I don't think so."

Naz couldn't believe what he was hearing. He had been bullied and picked on for many years and the very people who were supposed to be helping him had now turned out to be the worst.

"But Miss you just heard him."

Mr. Kelly looked at Naz with a smug grin and the fear in Naz turned to anger. He had never felt so much hatred for someone in his whole life. Naz snapped. He grabbed one of Mr. Kelly's fingers and pulled it back as hard as he could. The grip was released from around his neck but Naz kept pulling it and soon Mr. Kelly was kneeling on the floor begging him to let go. Miss Ferrie was also begging him to let go. Naz snapped it back with a force, cracking the bone.

"I'm going to kill you, you little Paki bastard." He shouted as he crumbled to the floor clutching his hand. Naz turned and ran. He ran out of the school and all the way home. Naz's father was outraged and had his coat on ready to march back up to the school with him. As they left the house a police car pulled up and Naz was charged with assault. He was thrown out of school once again and told to attend a panel hearing. The panel is a place were volunteers from the community, social workers, parents and teachers sit around a table and discuss what is the best punishment for youngsters who have found themselves in trouble. On deciding Naz's future, other teachers who were not present at the time of the assault had now come forward to tell a fictional report of what happened. Mr. Kelly's injuries were somewhat exaggerated to the extent that he claimed he couldn't use his hand again properly. Naz was made out to be a thug that was fast becoming out of control. The panel had believed the teachers version of events. Why wouldn't they? He had been transferred from so many schools. His parents were now starting to doubt him. The panel decided that a short spell in a Young Offenders Institution would maybe help control his violent temper. Jay had read Naz's file a number of times before stepping in. He did a background check on Mr. Kelly, something the children's panel never bothered to do. He found that he had a small file of complaints against him from previous students accusing him of bullying them. He was confused as to why a boy who worked hard, had top grades in every class he attended and who had never been in trouble outside of school, would suddenly attack a teacher for no reason, something didn't add up.

He tried to speak to Naz's parents and get them to appeal the decision but they had washed their hands of him and believed that a spell in Borstal would maybe sort him out. Although Jay couldn't change the panel's decision he fought hard and his request was granted to transfer Naz on to The Program.

5.

Christopher, or Topher as he preferred to be known, was going to be Jay's biggest challenge. Topher was not a fighter, he didn't have a hard upbringing, he hadn't committed any serious crime but he had constantly been in trouble since he was a very young age. His minor crimes were consistent enough to be put in front of the panel, many times. Each time he had been given a warning and was on his last chance but one day his last chance had run out and he was placed in a Y.O.I. Topher due to his size was being beat up on a daily basis by the other boys at the Institution until Dylan arrived and took him under his wing. Jay had turned up at the Institution to visit Dylan prior to the program being started and Dylan had asked Jay to look at Topher's file. Dylan was scared for Topher if he left. On reading his file, Jay had noticed that each report on him had stated that he was easily led. He had came from a good family who had went to great lengths to help him, but Topher continued to get himself in trouble which led to him being sent to the Institution. When Jay met Topher he found him to be a funny, likeable boy. The first thing he saw was his large innocent smile which he found unusual for someone who was constantly in trouble. The boys that Jay came across in the past with a record like Topher's would usually have a swagger and an attitude that he could relate to, but not Topher. He was the type of boy where everything in life was about having fun. He could understand now why he was given chance after chance from the authorities. In each case Topher pleaded that he was just in the wrong place at the wrong time and now after meeting him he could see why he would be believed. Topher had always appeared to latch onto the wrong crowd. The type of boys who had a bad upbringing, the ones you could tell straight off that they were destined for a life of crime. Most of these boys were stealing and breaking into places as they had nothing and had come from families with the same lifestyle. But Topher was different, his family always provided everything he ever needed. One of the reports that made Jay request Topher for the program was by a social worker, who, many years ago, had stated that Topher was not easily led but that he was the leader. He was an intelligent boy who had specifically picked out friends that made him appear to be the one led astray. Whatever the situation was, he knew Topher would be a difficult case to crack. He was either a naïve boy who needed some direction or a very intelligent boy with a total disregard for any figure of authority.

   Jay was handed another large stack of files from his assistant. He sat down at his desk and worked his way through them. Most had been put in a pile to be returned and occasionally there would be one that needed further reading. When he came across Stuart's file he glanced at the boy's record and was ready to put it aside until he read more. Stuart was the stereotypical hard case. He came from a family of petty criminals. His father and older brothers had or were still doing time in jail and Stuart would soon be following them. Most boys with files like Stuart's wouldn't be given a second look. He would put the files aside as he knew that most of them would think the program was just an easy way out from Borstal. With these types of boys, Jay could spend two years on the program with them and they would still leave to go and begin a life of crime. Jay had been around long enough to know if a person had an attitude that was capable of being changed. If the program was to be successful, Jay needed a boy who looked to be beyond help and Stuart's whole life of crime had been all mapped out since the day he was born. As he picked up the file he knew Stuart's family from his own past life of crime. The more he read the more he came to relate to the boy. Stuart had top grades when he was at school. Although he was always in trouble outside of school his reports from teachers were good enough to persuade Jay that he wanted Stuart on the program. If he could get through to someone like Stuart, maybe his influence could rub off on some of the other boys. Stuart had seen at first hand what a life of crime actually involved. As a young child he was taken by his mother to visit his father in many different prisons around Scotland. As he got older he was making the same trips to visit his older brothers. If Jay managed to turn someone like Stuart's life around the program would be a success. He would then, perhaps, get the funding for a further five years.

6.

At dinner that first night after Adam arrived, Jay introduced each of the other boys as they sat around the table and in turn they nodded their head in Adam's direction. The dinner was served by Topher and Naz. They all had turns each night of cooking. It was simple meals but it gave the boys some sort of responsibility while learning to do things for themselves. They all loved it when it was Naz's turn as he would always cook some special Indian curry. The boys were paired off alternatively so that they worked with someone different each time. The only two who had not worked together were Naz and Casey. Jay knew he needed more time to work on Casey's racist attitude before putting them together.

Later that night Jay had organised a discussion group. Each week they all sat down together and talked about anything that was bothering them on the program and put forward anything they would like to see happen on the program. This was intended to be a serious discussion but most of the time it ended in Jay laughing with the boys as they moaned about each others annoying habits.

"I would like to make a complaint about Dylan." Topher said.

"What! What have I done now?"

"Hold it Dylan, let him speak. That's what the discussion group is for." Jay says.

"I would like to request Dylan be made to sleep in the other dorm on his own"

"Yeah, me too. I mean we all have to fart but my bunk is straight across from Dylan's and he wafts the covers so that the smell comes directly to me." Casey says.

"Guys, it's only when you feed me soup for lunch, if you put too much vegetables in there, they make me fart." Dylan pleads.

"Yeah but you don't have to waft it in my face."

"Well I don't want it to linger about in my bed, do I?" Jay laughs but his smile drops when he looks at Adam who has no expression.

"What do you think Adam, how do you suppose we resolve this?" Jay says trying to get Adam involved. Adam looks around the room at everyone as they stare at him.

"Stop feeding the big dopey retard then." He says as he smiles at Dylan.

They all laugh as Dylan grabs Adam and puts him in a head lock and they playfully wrestle around the room. Jay sits back smiling with the thought that Adam will fit in well with the other boys.

Over the next few days Adam began to settle in on the program but realised the busy work schedule and educational side of the program was not what he was expecting. Adam noticed that most of the boys went out of their way to make him feel welcome, except Stuart. When Ritchie who had been the "I've never cooked anything in my life."

"It's easy mate, I'll do most of it but I'll sprevious leader of the boys left, Jay thought it would be a good idea to nominate Stuart to take over. This meant that he was now responsible for giving out the work details for the week and making sure the rest of the boys were doing their chores properly.

On Adam's first night of making dinner for everyone he was paired off with Topher. As Topher got on with the task Adam stood around reluctant to help.

"I'm not here to cook for everyone."

"Hey we are all here to muck in and help each other, everyone has to take a turn."
how you things as we go. Here you can chop these tomatoes, you know how to chop tomatoes don't you?"

"What's this place all about? How is learning to cook going to stop anybody from getting into trouble?"

"Hey Adam we are all here for the same reasons you are. What was it? A broken home, in with the wrong crowd, petty crime, stealing, drugs, fighting, stabbing…
Adam looks up at Topher as he mentions stabbing.

"Stabbing" Topher says again as he looks at Adam.

"Well I never actually…" Adam attempts to plead his case when Topher interrupts by reaching over and taking the kitchen knife from him.
"I'll just get you to grate some cheese, that okay?" Topher says quite seriously.

They both look at each other and start laughing as Adam realises Topher is only winding him up.

Later the next day the English teacher arrives so the boys gather in the classroom. As the boys are at different levels of education they are all left to carry on with their own work and the teacher comes around individually to see them. Adam sits at the back and the teacher introduces herself. She has never met Adam and asks him to complete a set of tasks to find out what level he is at. Adam completes the tests in half the time allocated and watches as away.

"Excuse me Adam but you were requested on this program so that we could try to educate you and teach you how to show some respect. This is for your benefit, to show the authorities that you are better than what they perceive you to be. We believe and trust that you are not the type of Casey reads to the rest of the boys.

He struggles with some of the more difficult words but is helped along by the teacher.

"Well done Casey, that's coming along. Adam you appear to have finished would you like to start where Casey finished off."

"Not really." Adam says looking person whose future lies in prison. Now take the book and start where Casey left off or I will inform Jay that you would like to spend the rest of your time in the Institution."

Adam stands up, walks to the front of the class and picks up the book from the table and begins to read faultlessly. He reads two paragraphs and puts the book down.

"Do you want me to continue?"

"No I think you've proved your point. Smart ass."

The teacher says smiling at Adam.

After looking at the results of Adams tests and hearing his reading skills he is started on the same course work as Stuart, who was until now considered the brain box of the group.

A few weeks had past and Adam was starting to fit in perfectly with life on the program. He began to trust Jay and saw him as more of a friend than a figure of authority. The only problem Adam had was the two security staff, Frank and Bruce. When these two were on together and Jay wasn't around Adam noticed the rest of the boys kept to themselves and became distant...Adam was about to find out why.

Jay was away to another meeting with the Board and Frank and Bruce were left in charge. The boys had finished their chores Jay had set them to do while he was away and were gathered in the lounge watching TV. Adam went into the kitchen to make himself a sandwich, when Frank appeared. He stood in the doorway and waited until Adam had finished then casually walked over, picked up his plate and tilted it until the sandwich fell on the floor.

"Oops." Frank says.

Adam looked at him confused.

"Pick it up then." Frank says staring at him.

Adam had seen that stare many times in the past. It usually meant trouble. So much violence and hatred flashed through Adam's mind. Adam stood rooted to the spot unsure of what this was all about. He squared up to Frank.

"Come on then. If you're going to do something, do it. Let's see how hard you think you really are." Frank says with his menacing eyes and smug grin.

Dylan walks into the kitchen.

"What's going on?" He says as he sees Adam and Frank with their faces only inches from each other.

Frank takes a step back and smiles at Adam.

"Clean it up." He says as he turns and walks out of the kitchen.

Dylan sees the rage in Adam's eyes and looks down at his clenched fists. Dylan bends down and picks up the sandwich.

"Don't let him get to you mate, that's what he wants." Dylan puts the sandwich in the bin and takes out the bread to make another.

"What the hell is that all about?"

"We don't know. They try it on with all of us; some of the other boys have been hit physically when no-one is around."

"Why don't you tell Jay?"

"We have, each one of us has mentioned it to him but because it happens when we are on our own it's our word against theirs. Jay knows what's going on and says he knows why they are doing it but he needs proof."

7.

After another pointless meeting with the Board Jay is in a rush to get out of the building and back to the camp. He knows the boys have been left under the supervision of Frank and Bruce, which means things could kick off big time. He has told the boys in secret not to be left alone in their company. He hasn't mentioned it to Adam though as he thought it best to let him settle in before letting him know what was going on. Jay is about to enter the lift when his newly acquired friend catches up with him. They don't speak until they enter the lift and the door closes.

"How is your evidence going?"

"Not so good, my boys are being bullied by security staff that I have no say over and I can't even make a formal complaint. As soon as I mention them at the meetings I am cut off by Williamson and none of you guys will speak to help me out. Does he not realise I am trying to help these boys"

"Look just hold tight and tell your boys to stay calm. I am working on it. If I am caught going behind Blair's back I'll be out of a job and my life won't be worth living."

The lift stops and so does the conversation. They stand apart as someone enters. The lift reaches the ground floor and as they all leave she slips a piece of paper into Jay's pocket.

On the way to the car park Jay puts his hand into his pocket for his car keys and finds the piece of paper.

Rich Bryson received £2000 in his bank account from

council funds and has been offered a permanent job in Councillor Williamson's department.

Jay stands outside of the minibus and reads the note over again before it sinks in. Williamson is paying Ritchie to keep his mouth shut. Two thousand is not a lot of money but to a sixteen year old it is a fortune. Jay knows he has to get back to the camp as soon as possible but makes a detour to pay Rich a little visit.

Prior to Rich leaving the program Jay had looked at his situation and was informed that he could not return home as his parents did not want him there. On leaving the program Jay set him up in a small flat and found him a job. As he was the first to leave the program it was imperative that Rich stayed on the straight and narrow.

Jay arrived at the flat and knocked on the door.

"Hi Jay, how's it going?"

"Can I have a word?"

"Sure, come in. Sounds serious"

Jay walks into the flat and straight away he clocks the new TV and stereo.

"Not working today?"

"No, I eh, handed in my notice. I have a new job, I start next week. I thought you would have known about it."

"Why would I know about it?"

"Well it's with the council. Some really big guy said he wanted to try and help out with the program and find us decent jobs."

"I see you've been treating yourself" Jay says nodding in the direction of the TV and stereo.

"Eh yeah, I eh got offered an advance if I took the job."

Through Jay's years of experience he was able to tell when someone was lying by their tone of voice, their actions or even just by the look in their eyes. He knew straight away that Rich was lying but he didn't push it. He wanted to ask him so many questions. Who approached him about the job? Who offered him the money? What has he promised to say or not to say?

"I need to ask you something Rich."

"Yeah, sure what's up?"

"The notes I took during our one to one sessions, you know, the ones I have locked away."

"Uh yeah, what about them?"

"You signed a complaints statement against Frank and Bruce do you remember?"

"Yeah, of course, but it was nothing really. I mean my head was really mixed up during those sessions."

Jay suddenly feels angry and betrayed as he realises someone has got to Rich and he could count him out as a witness. More important to him is just how much he has said about the complaints book. Williamson has obviously covered himself with the bribe by calling it an advance. He now has other things to worry about. Rich's new job, how long will he last before he is set up for stealing or some other petty crime? Jay gets up to leave and realises he has to do something soon.

"Oh, Rich, you wouldn't happen to have mentioned those notes to anyone else would you?"

"No, why would I?"

Jay looks straight at Rich; another lie.

The sun is shining when Jay arrives back at the camp but the boys are all inside. He walks straight to his office and takes out his key to unlock it. Dylan walks past and gives him a look and then nods in the direction of Adam.

"Adam can I see you in here for a minute." Jay says. Adam walks from the lounge and follows Jay into the office.

"Take a seat."

"What's this about?"

"Is there anything you want to tell me?"

"No, why?"

"Did anything happen today that I should know about?" Adam is a bit confused as he has never been one to open his mouth, he would usually deal with things in his own way. In the few weeks that he has been on the program, Adam has given Jay a lot of respect and has begun to put his trust in him. Adam looks around the office, at the walls, the ceiling and back to the walls before eventually locking eyes
with Jay.

"What do you mean? Are you referring to the incident in the kitchen earlier where one of your security wardens was close to getting his face smashed in. If you are referring to that then yeah I think maybe you should know about it." Jay sits back in his chair.

"I'm really sorry Adam. I should have told you what was going on. It's been happening to all the boys here. They are employed by a separate department from The Program. I know who's behind it but I can't prove it just yet. It would be in their best interest if this program failed."

"Is there anything we could do?"

"Yes, nothing. I really need you guys to try to control yourselves and not kick off if they start."

"I have a lot of respect for you Jay and I can see what you're trying to do for us with the program and all but I'm sorry. I can't promise that, all I can say is that I'll try my best."

"That's all I ask."

During the night Dylan gets up to use the bathroom. As he stands relieving himself Bruce enters. He walks over to

Dylan and pushes him from behind. This results in Dylan dribbling on himself and the floor.

"Look what you've gone and done, you big retard." Bruce says with a smug grin.

Dylan looks at him but does nothing. Bruce pushes him again and Dylan stumbles back slipping in his own urine and falls to the floor. Bruce kicks him in the stomach and slaps him in the head.

"Look at the mess you've made retard. Clean it up."
Bruce grabs his hair and pushes his face to the floor.

"Come on then retard."

Dylan lies there gritting his teeth and clenching his fists. He feels ready to explode. There's only so much he can take.

The handle on the door makes a noise and Bruce stands up and takes a step back. Adam enters.

"What's going on? Are you okay Dylan?"
Adam can see the rage in Dylan's eyes.

"He's fine, he's had a bit of an accident. Clean yourself up and get back to bed." Bruce says as he goes to walk out of the bathroom.

Dylan watches as Adam squares up to Bruce on his way out. Bruce smirks and walks past him. Adam picks up a towel, throws it on the floor and offers his hand to help Dylan up.

"Thanks mate."

"No problem, I owed you one."

They both clean up and head back to their beds. In the morning Frank leaves and is replaced by Jack who is welcomed with big smiles from all the boys.

On finishing his shift at the camp Frank is ordered to attend a meeting with his boss at the council offices. He walks into the reception and is met by the long faces of Williamson's unhappy workforce. The receptionist announces on the phone that he has arrived and he is ushered through.

"What the hell is going on at that camp? I've been expecting to hear news that one of those little brats has lashed out and attacked one of you. But all I ever hear is growing reports of how they are passing exams and behaving like choir boys. I paid you and your sidekick to do a job, now why haven't you done it."

"We've tried, they won't react. Jay must know what's going on and warned them."

"Well I guess we will have to go to plan B."

"What's plan B?"

"Jason Fallon"

"What, we start on him?"

"No, those boys will start on him and you and Bruce will witness it. If you know what I mean"

"You mean we do some damage and blame it on them."

"Now you're getting it."

"But that means we would have to do a proper job so that he won't be capable of defending them."

"If that's what it takes."

"Wait a minute; we never agreed to go as far as this." Williamson throws a fat envelope on his desk. Frank leans over and picks it up. He looks inside and smiles.

"I think that will cover it."

"Oh just so that you know, he has a notebook filled with complaints about you and Bruce. Each and every time you did anything to those boys has been recorded, dated and signed by each boy."

"What? You've got to be joking?"

"No. So I suggest you get hold of that before you do anything."

"How do you know all this?"
"From our newly acquired employee"
"Rich."
They both smile at each other and Frank walks out of the office holding the envelope tightly.

8.

Over the next week Jay had been putting his evidence together and was about to go above Williamson's head with his complaints. On the morning of the shift change over, Jack was replaced by Bruce. Jay noticed that Jack was acting very strange. He tried to get him on his own to talk but as Bruce arrived, Jack left without saying a word. There was a trip planned into town that day as Jay promised Adam he would get him kitted out with some new clothes. Jay had done this for some of the other boys who had arrived at the camp with little more than the clothes on their back. He could tell Frank and Bruce were up to something and decided to take all the boys into town with him.

The boys only ever left the camp for specific reasons and it was usually to help with shopping or visits with their families. For them all to be together on a trip into town was a big deal for them. There was the usual teasing and wind-ups between the boys during the journey but it was all in good fun. Jay could see that the boys were happy and excited to be away from the camp for the day. After a quick shopping spree where Adam was constantly teased for his chosen attire Jay decided to treat them to lunch. With large plates of junk food all around Jay sat back in his chair and watched as the boys laughed and joked among themselves. Just over six months ago some of these boys were destined for a term in Borstal where they would have more than likely come out with more criminal intent than before they went in. He knows he has chosen the correct boys for the program although Casey's racist attitude is still a problem. But that can be dealt with over time. Jay treats them to another round of drinks before they walk back through the town towards the mini bus. The boys are quiet on the journey home and Jay knows it is because they are about to be faced with Frank and Bruce. With the effort that these boys have shown he knows he has to do something soon.

They arrive back at the camp and Jay heads straight to his office. As soon as he sits down at his desk he knows that something is not right. He notices that some things have been moved around and the drawers have been upturned. The locks on his filling cabinet have been forced open and he searches for his secret complaints book. It is gone. He is ready to storm out and confront Frank and Bruce but he stands and takes many deep breaths until he calms down. The last thing he wants is for his boys to see him become angry and aggressive after everything he has tried to teach them. He makes a decision to wait until the morning and confront the Board with what evidence he has and ask for an investigation. Jay makes a phone call and catches the council offices before closing. He requests an emergency meeting with the Board for the next morning and the message is passed on to Williamson.

"Is everything okay Jay?" Dylan says as he appears from his office.

"Yeah, sure, why?"

"You look a little stressed."

"No, I'm fine; I just have a few things on my mind." Jay says looking over at the two wardens as they whisper between themselves.

"Oh right, I see what you mean."

During the evening Frank receives an anonymous phone call where he is informed about the emergency meeting. He is told that whatever it takes the meeting must not take place.

Only a few hours after going to bed Adam wakens with a sudden urge to use the toilet. He stumbles through the dark until he reaches the hallway. As he walks through to the bathroom he overhears some raised voices from Jay's office. On the way back he creeps lightly towards the office door and hears some dull noises and a low whimpering.

"Where is it?" Bruce says in an angry tone.

Another dull smacking sound and then a whimper.

Adam opens the door handle slowly and peaks around. Frank and Bruce have their backs to the door and through the gap Adam can see Jay tied to his chair with a rag shoved in his mouth. His face is swollen and blood is dripping down from his head. Adam is frozen to the spot and looks on in shock. Bruce raises a steel bar and holds it in front of Jays face.

"You have one last chance. Where is the notebook?" Jay sees Adam through the gap and they lock eyes with each other. Bruce takes a large swing with the bar and it crunches into the side of Jays head. Jay's head snaps to the side as the blood splatters against the wall. Adam opens the door further and Frank turns to see him standing with his eyes wide and his mouth open. Frank reaches over and grabs Adam by his t-shirt. Adam steps back and pulls the door closed on his arm. He keeps a tight grip on his t-shirt but Adam leans forward and sinks his teeth into the back of Frank's hand making him release his grip. Adam runs across the hall and back into the boys' dorm. He puts on the light and runs towards his bunk and starts to push it towards the door. At the same time the rest of the boys wake up.

"Come on, help me." He shouts.

Dylan gets up and helps him without even questioning why. The metal bunk is slammed tight against the door and Adam goes to grab another.

"What's going on?" Stuart demands.

"Frank and Bruce, they've just smashed Jay he's covered in blood. Come on help me"

Frank tries to open the door and the first bunk is pushed slightly forward.

"Open the door." Frank shouts.

With the help of Bruce they give the door a large shove and it opens enough for Frank to slide his head through.

"Move the bed or I'll kill the lot of you."

Casey takes a run from the other side of the room and Frank slides his head back just in time as the bed is forced back closing the door again. Dylan, Adam and Topher manage to pick up another bunk and throw it on top of the first one. The rest of the boys push all the beds towards the door barricading themselves inside.

"What do we do now?" Naz says.

"Get something on your feet we'll make a run for it." Adam says.

"Wait a minute, I'm going nowhere I haven't done anything wrong." Stuart says.

"Well you can stay here and tell them that, but I'm going."

"How are you planning to get out of here?"

Adam looks up at the windows which are high up and only two foot square.

"You've got to be kidding."

As the boys quickly put on their jeans and trainers Frank

and Bruce are taking it in turns to barge the door and the beds are moving slightly each time.

As soon as the boys are ready Adam gets the boys to pile up their lockers near the window. Casey notices the door being opened further and Frank's arm is through the gap. He grabs Dylan and they both run forward and push the beds back squashing Franks arm in the process. He lets out a loud yelp before he manages to slide it back through. The boys take it in turns to help each other climb out of the window. Frank and Bruce start charging the door at the same time and Casey is the last one trying to hold the beds in place. His heels start sliding backwards with each push.

"Come on you guys hurry up; I can't hold it much longer."

The door opens enough for Frank to fit through and Casey makes a run for it. He climbs up the lockers against the wall and reaches for the window.

As he pulls himself up onto the ledge Frank grabs his leg.

"Guys he's got my leg, help."

"Come on Dylan." Naz shouts as he runs back to the window.

Dylan stands with his back against the wall with his hands clenched together. Naz puts his foot onto Dylan's grasp and lifts himself up to the window. He grabs Casey's hands and pulls him. Frank has a tight hold on Casey's leg but as he is balancing on the lockers he has no support. Casey uses his other leg and keeps kicking back as hard as he could. One eventually lands on Frank's chest pushing him off balance. He lets go of Casey trying to control his fall. Casey stumbles out of the window and they all land in a pile on the ground. They waste no time in getting up and running as fast as they can through the dark fields away from the camp.

Bruce calls the police and they are immediately alerted to be on the look out for six teenage boys. Before the ambulance arrives Frank wipes down any fingerprints on the steel bar and anything else that they could have touched while they were in Jay's office. Bruce puts his head down to Jay's face.

"He's still breathing."
"Well?"
"Well what?"
"What are you waiting on?"
Bruce hesitates and then looks up at Frank.
"Out of the way" Franks says.

He moves down towards Jay and puts his hand over his mouth and nose. Bruce stands up and watches as Jay's body jerks slightly several times before Frank gets up and walks to the bathroom to wash the blood off his hands. Bruce follows him as they discuss their version of events so that their stories coincide.

A police car pulls up and the ambulance arrives only minutes later. They go straight to work untying him from the chair and giving him shock treatment as he lies on the floor of his office. Frank and Bruce look on from the hall outside as Jay is pronounced dead at the scene.

Detective Chief Inspector Smith is woken with the news that Jason Fallon has been attacked and killed by the boys in his care. He gets out of bed and instead of his usual ritual of two mugs of strong coffee to help him face his daily events he quickly gets dressed and rushes out the door. He had known Jay for many years after he had contacted him for advice on various social work projects. He also had the opportunity to work along side him and witnessed first hand the respect some of the most vulnerable teenagers had for him. He found the news of his

murder quite disturbing. As soon as he arrived on the scene he was introduced to Frank and Bruce and immediately took a dislike to them. He, like Jay had been around long enough to know when someone was lying.
When Smith arrived back at the station he listened to the fictional statements of Frank and Bruce when interviewed.

"So you woke during the night to hear a noise coming from Jason's office. When you opened the door he was tied to a chair and one of the boys, Adam was it?"

"Yeah"

"Hit him over the head with a steel bar."
That's when the other boys in the office turned on you. You went to alert your partner and upon returning the boys had run to their dorm and barricaded themselves in using the metal bunks. You managed to get the door open but they climbed through the window."

"Yeah, that's right." Frank says.
D.C.I. Smith terminates the interview and walks out the room with his partner. Detective Constable Nevin.

"What do you think?" She says.

Smith gives her a puzzled look and says "I think we have to find those boys."

9.

In the darkness the boys ran through the muddy fields and woodland and eventually stopped to catch their breath. They did not know where they were as the only light to guide them was from the moon. They could hear the police and ambulance sirens in the distance but they had run too far now to see them.

"I hope Jay is going to be okay." Dylan says.
"I know I hope they haven't killed him." Adam says.
"I thought they were going to kill me." Casey says.
"Yeah, you're lucky me and Naz reacted when we did."
"Yeah, thanks Dylan."
"What about Naz?"
Casey hesitates for a second.
"Oh, eh thanks."
"No problem, I maybe won't be so quick next time."
"So what did you actually see Adam?" Stuart says.
"They had him tied to a chair and his face was banged up pretty bad. They were asking about some book. He saw me looking from around the door then Bruce smashed him in the head with a metal bar."
"It will be the complaints book, they must have found out about it."
"What are we going to do Stuart?" Dylan asks.
"I think we need to find out how Jay is first. If he's okay we've nothing to worry about."
"And if he's not okay."
"Well then we're in a lot of trouble."

"Why? We haven't done anything wrong." Naz says.

"That's not the way Frank and Bruce will tell it."

"What do you mean? They won't believe them… Will they?"

"What? They won't believe two security wardens over six teenage boys who all have criminal records and have done or were about to do time in Borstal."

"I never really thought about it like that." Naz says looking to the ground as his mind wanders into his own little world.

"I think we should keep walking until we can find a place to hide. When the sun comes up we'll get to a phone and find out what's happening." Stuart says letting the rest of the boys know he's in charge.

The boys trudge through more muddy fields and head for a light they can see in the distance. It is a security light fitted on the side of a remote farmhouse. There are large sheds and barns close by and Stuart leads the way as they open them to check what's inside. He finds one that is stacked with hay and walks in the darkness to the back of the barn. Some of the boys find places to curl up while the others lie back in total silence and stare up at the roof. They all eventually nod off to sleep but Adam is woken a few hours later by someone moving around outside the barn. He hears the tractor starting up and driving off. There is a small light coming in through holes in the roof and Adam decides to get up and have a look around.

"Where are you going?" Topher whispers.

"I'm just away to check things out and have a look around."

"Good, I'll come with you."

Topher moves quietly so as not to waken the other boys. The sun is rising as they leave the barn and they head straight for the farmer's house.

"Wait Adam, what if the family are up and about."

"Then we'll go back."

They creep around to the back of the house and as Adam looks in to the kitchen window Topher is opening the back door.

"Can you see anyone?" He whispers to Adam.

"No"

They enter the kitchen and Topher takes out the bread from the bread bin and casually walks over to the fridge.

"There's no butter they've only got margarine." he says as he continues to take out a block of cheese and some ham.

Adam is busy looking in drawers and cupboards. He looks around at Topher who is busy spreading two slices of bread.

"What are you doing?"

"Making myself a sandwich"

"We don't have time for that."

Adam finds what he is looking for, a large carrier bag.

"Put that stuff back in the fridge. Put the bread in this bag and any other loose food that we can all eat."

"What do you mean loose food?"

"Crisps, biscuits or bottles of juice"

"Where are you going?"

"To find a phone"

Adam walks through the kitchen into the lounge and finds a phone near the window.

"Kathy it's Adam."

"Hi Adam, what time is it? Is everything okay?"

Jay had tracked down Kathy when he had joined the program and Adam had visited her weekly and phoned her every other day since.

"It's early Kathy. I need a favour, there's been some trouble at The Program and Jay's been hurt. I need you to find out if he's okay."

"What kind of trouble?"

"I saw him being beaten up by the security wardens. They chased us and we think they are going to try and blame it on us. I need you to find out how bad it is."

Adam hears movement from upstairs.

"I have to go now but I'll phone back as soon as I can."

Adam hangs up the phone and goes back to the kitchen. He finds Topher sitting at the table finishing his sandwich and drinking a large glass of milk.

"We've got to go, someone's upstairs." Adam whispers. Topher drinks his glass of milk in one go and walks over to the sink to wash it.

"What are you doing? Come on."

Adam can't help but laugh at Topher who is more concerned about cleaning up after himself than being caught in someone's house. He picks up the carrier bag and they walk out the back door and back to the barn.

"Hey guys, we have your breakfast." Topher says wakening up the rest of the boys.

"Where did you get all this?" Stuart says looking on as Topher empties the bag.

"From the house just outside" Adam says.

"That's good, did you not think of telling us you were going?"

"You lot were all sleeping, what's the problem?"

"Because we don't know what's going on with Jay and when the farmer realises his house has been broken into there will be police all over here."

"Don't worry about it, we didn't break in. The door was open and any mess we made Topher cleaned up. Actually

the place is probably cleaner now than before we went in." Adam says looking at Topher as they both laugh.
Stuart squares up to Adam.

"What? Do you think this is funny?" Stuart says.

Adam's smile drops and he squares up to Stuart. Dylan steps forward and wedges himself in between them.

"Come on you guys, the last thing we need is to be fighting amongst ourselves. Lets eat this and we'll go and find out what the story is with Jay."

"Yeah, come on guys." Naz says as he stands up and pulls Adams arm to sit down.

"In Jay's absence, I'm in charge and I make the decisions." Stuart demands.

"We know mate, just sit down and forget it."
Stuart sits down and Casey passes him some bread.

"Adam you know whenever Jay left the camp, he always left someone in charge, and he nominated Stuart." Dylan informs him.

Adam doesn't say anything but shrugs his shoulders and picks up a piece of bread.

The boys polish off most of the stolen food and Stuart decides that it is not safe to stay in the barn. He leads the way back through the same muddy fields that they hiked through last night. As the get closer to the camp they take a different route and walk towards Dundee.

"I'm hungry again." Dylan says.

"You're always hungry." Casey replies.

"But we've been walking for ages now and I've worked up an appetite. I need some food."

"Look there's a shop up ahead." Casey says as he sees a small local convenience store.

"What, did you bring your wallet with you?" Stuart says.

"No, but a small shop like that has got to be run by Pakis

and Naz is probably related. They all are. So he can go in and get us sorted out." Casey says.

"No we're not all related because were not all Pakistani's. My parents are Indian. And even if I was related and you were dying of hunger you're the last person I would go and get food for."

"Ah don't you two start again. Look if we can get to a phone I'll find out about Jay then if it's safe we can all head back to the camp." Stuart says.

"You guys can look for a phone; I'm going for some food." Dylan says storming off in the direction of the shop.

"Yeah me too, I'm with Dylan, and besides the Paki will probably have a phone anyway." Casey says as he runs off before Naz can say anything back to him.

"Yeah you're right we should head for the shop. They'll probably have a phone there. Come on guys."

Stuart says as walks off trying to save face as the leader. The other boys look at each other and smile as they walk behind him knowing full well his role of leader has just been tested. The boys walk into the shop together and separate when they go down the small isles.

"I told you it was a Paki shop." Casey whispers to Naz before ducking under a shelf.

"It's Pakistani not Paki." Naz says angrily.
Stuart approaches the shop owner who stands nervously behind the counter and politely asks if he could use his telephone. The shop owner looks him up and down and then scans the shop for the rest of the boys.

"You boys are in real trouble." He says.

"What do you mean?"
The owner doesn't answer as he marches out from behind the counter and down the isle. He grabs Casey by the arm and pulls out a packet of biscuits from under his t-shirt.

"Get out of my shop you little thieves, the lot of you. Get out."

Dylan looks over at the freezer.

"Look guys choc ices." He says as he opens the lid and takes one out.

"Put that back" The owner shouts.

Dylan throws one across the shop to Topher who opens the wrapper and bites into it.

"Mm, not bad"

"Guys what are you doing, Jay will go nuts." Stuart pleads.

The boys run around the shop helping themselves, as the owner chases them and tries to throw them out. While all this commotion is going on, Adam sneaks behind the counter and picks up the phone. He quickly dials Kathy's number.

"It's Adam. I only have a few seconds. What's the news on Jay."

"Oh Adam it's been on the radio all morning. Jay has been murdered and the police say they are looking for six teenage boys in connection with it. Adam I…"

The line goes dead.

"Get out of my shop." The owner says as he looks over the counter down at Adam who is crouched on the floor. The owner has pulled the plug out of the phone. Adam puts down the receiver and sits there for a few seconds taking in the news. He stands up and looks at Dylan who has a carrier bag in one hand and is filling it with the other. They lock eyes and Adam shakes his head slightly. Dylan knows straight away that something is wrong.

"Is it Jay?"

Adam nods

"Is he dead?"

Adam nods again. Dylan lets go of the bag and his eyes widen. The owner grabs Dylan and pushes him towards the door.

"Get out, get out." He shouts.

Dylan turns and pushes the owner back. The owner grabs Dylan and puts him in a head lock. They stumble around the shop knocking over shelves and display stalls before Dylan falls to his knees. The owner tightens his grip and Dylan is about to pass out when Adam picks up a bottle of beer from behind the counter and runs towards them. He smashes it over the owners head and he releases his grip from around Dylan's neck.

"Come on, we've got to get out of here." Stuart shouts. The boys all run to the door but Dylan still coughing and struggling to regain his breathing walks back and picks up the bag of food. Adam shakes his head as he waits holding the door open.

10.

The boys run through a large part of waste ground until they reach a small wooded area. Stuart, who is leading the way, stops once he thinks they are in deep enough that passers-by won't see them. Dylan passes around the bag of stolen food.

"Are you not having any Dylan?" Topher asks.

"Nah, I'm not really hungry anymore."

"Why what's wrong?"

Dylan looks at Adam and nods at him to tell them. Topher looks at Adam

"What's going on?"

"I have something to tell you." Adam says.

"We kind of gathered that, what is it?"

"It's about Jay."

They all stop eating and look at Adam knowing they are about to hear bad news.

"He's dead. They killed him."

The boys all stare at each other shaking their heads in disbelief.

"How did you find out?" Stuart asks.

"I made a phone call from the shop."

"Who did you phone?"

"My old foster mother. She said it's been on the radio all morning and the police are looking for six teenage boys."

"What, they think we done it?" Naz asks.

"She never said. She just said she we are wanted in connection with it."

"Of course they think we done it. Frank and Bruce are not exactly going to admit that they done it are they." Casey says.

"I don't feel hungry anymore either." Naz says throwing the food on the ground.

"So where do we go from here?" Casey asks.

The boys in turn, all look at Stuart."

"Why are you all looking at me?"

Because Jay nominated you leader remember?" Topher says.

Stuart pauses for a minute.

"I guess we go back and explain what happened. Let them know the truth."

The boys sit in silence for a long time as they think about the prospect of going back to face Frank and Bruce and also the thought of being sent back to Borstal.

"You know they're never going to believe us don't you." Adam says.

"Well what do you suggest we do?" Stuart says hating that Adam has said what was on everyone's mind.

"Find Jack he'll know what to do."

"Yeah, Jack. He'll help us. That sounds good to me. Yeah let's go find Jack." Casey says.

The boys' faces light up and they look at Stuart for his decision.

"And how are we supposed to find him. We don't even know where he lives."

"I do." Dylan says.

The boys all look at Dylan.

"And how do you know that?"

"Jay left me in his office once, a while back and I read some files. I remembered Jack's address because it wasn't far from where I used to live."

"If it was a while ago what's to say he hasn't moved since then?"

"What's to say he has?" Adam quickly replies.

"Come on Stuart, it's our only hope. Unless you want to go back and face being charged with Jay's murder" Casey says.

Stuart doesn't take long to think about this as he looks at the faces staring at him. He realises that if he decides to hand himself in, he'll be doing it alone.

"Right we'll go, but we'll have to wait here until it gets dark. I don't think it would be wise for us to walk about in broad daylight if they are looking for six teenage boys."

***

"What do you mean you couldn't find the book?" Williamson shouts as Frank and Bruce stand rooted to the spot in his office. Both of them feeling like schoolboys getting a telling off from their teacher.

"Blair...eh Councillor Williamson, we turned that office upside down. There's no way he wouldn't tell us after the beating we gave him." Frank pleads.

"Who else had access to that office?"

"No one"

"What about Jack?"

Frank and Bruce look at each other and back to Williamson.

"I think you two had better get around there before that book ends up in the wrong hands." Williamson threatens. Both men walk towards the door and as Bruce opens it slightly and with one foot touching the marbled floor in the reception, Williamson shouts.

"You better get that book, whatever it takes."

Williamson's ranting was nothing new to the other council staff in the building that overheard him. All except one ignored it. Williamson's personal assistant, who was busy at her desk and heard every word. She knew exactly what book he was referring to. She was handed the book the night before. As the two employees in their security uniforms walked past her desk her heart skipped a beat. She knew where they were heading and she knew she had to get out of the office to make a phone call. If she phoned from her desk if would be traced back to her. She watched as the two men entered the lift and the doors closed. She gathered some papers and walked casually over to press the lift button. Flicking through the papers in her arm as though they were important documents she glanced at the numbers up above as they went to zero and slowly came back up to four. She entered the lift and as soon as the door opened on the bottom floor she walked as fast as she could to the nearest phone box. Her hands were shaking as she dialled the number…no answer. She dialled again… no answer. Where could he be? Hopefully he won't be home until after they've been. She heard Williamson loud and clear. His two goons were told 'whatever it takes.' She knew that meant Jack could be hurt. Jack had never hurt anybody in his life. There wasn't a bad bone in his body. When he got out of the army and came to his sister for a job she didn't hesitate to pull some strings to help him. He was her kid brother. She had been married and had a different last name so nobody knew that they were related. She knew he would be great with those kids but at the same time she was using him to keep her informed about the program. In a way she felt she was no better than Williamson. If anything happened to Jack, it would be on her conscience. What was worrying her now was that Jack could tell them who he passed the book on to. She hung up the receiver and quickly walked to the car park. She was soon speeding out of the city centre towards Jack's house.

There was a car parked outside when she arrived so she pulled up further along the street and waited. Several minutes later Jack's front door opened and Frank and Bruce walked out. She pulled out a note pad from her handbag and recorded the time. They sped off and past her on the way. She got out of her car and walked the short distance across the road hoping and praying that Jack wasn't in. The front door appeared to be unlocked but after a closer inspection she noticed it had been burst open.

"Jack. Jack are you there?" She shouts as she enters the hallway.

A quick glance into the living room and she notices the place had been turned over. Her heart starts to beat faster and her legs begin to shake as she walks up the stairs.

"Jack. Jack its Heather."
She slowly opens his bedroom door to Jack lying face down on his bed. Her worst fear had come true. She leans over him and turns his head to the side. She puts her hand to her mouth in shock and feels like she is about to vomit. There is a thin red line going around his neck revealing to her that he has been strangled. There are also finger marks where it looks as though he has tried to release whatever material they used. She feels for a pulse…nothing.

She hurry's out of the house and back to her car. She only drives a short distance and has to stop. Her stomach starts to retch and she opens her door to vomit. She hadn't eaten today so the retching brings up nothing. With her eyes bulging and tears flowing she makes her way home. She wants to go to the police but that would mean giving a statement against Williamson and handing over all the evidence she has gathered. She feels that she is not ready to do that yet. Heather doesn't know who to trust as Williamson has bought over so many people. She takes deep breaths and drives to a friend's house. Sammi had been her friend since they were young and had been there and helped her through the break up of her marriage.

"What's wrong? What's happened?" Sammi says upon seeing her friend in such a distressed state.

She ushers her inside and once she has calmed down her friend tells her what's happened. The first thing Sammi does is go outside and open her garage doors to put heather's car inside and hide it in case they come looking for her. Sammi arranges for her husband to go to Heather's home and collect some of her things warning him to make sure he is not followed. Heather wants to report the murder but Sammi persuades her that they should leave it until later in the hope that someone else discovers it. If they didn't hear anything by nine o' clock that night her friend would drive to a phone box at the other end of town and make an anonymous call. As soon as Jack's body is discovered Williamson will find out that they are related.

***

It began to get dark around eight o' clock and Stuart noticed the rest of the boys were beginning to get restless.

"Come on Stuart. What are we waiting on?" Casey asks.

"Yeah Stuart, if we leave it too late it will look even more suspicious if the six of us are wandering around at night." Dylan says.

Stuart starts to think about this and makes a decision.

"Okay let's go. Dylan you lead the way as you're the only one who knows where he lives."

Dylan walks off with Adam and Topher at either side of him and leads the boys through mostly quiet back streets whenever possible and hides if anything resembles a police car. Upon reaching Jack's street Dylan leads the boys down a dark path. This runs parallel with the street's back gardens. Dylan stops halfway down the path and tells the rest of the boys to wait.

"Where are you going?" Stuart says.

"I have to find out which one is Jack's."

Dylan climbs a fence and walks to the front of the house. He was at number seven and Jack's was eleven.

"Two doors down guys."

The boys make their way over Jack's fence and Stuart is in front as they approach Jack's front door.

"It doesn't look as though he's in. There's no light on."

"Just knock anyway." Dylan says.

Stuart knocks on the door and it slides open.

"Guys the doors open."

"Go in then."

"I'm not away to walk into his house."

"Topher." Dylan whispers loudly.

Topher casually walks up the steps and into the house putting on the lights as he goes.

"What a tip. Does Jack never clean up after himself?" Topher comments on seeing the living room.

"It looks as though he's been doing a bit of decorating." Casey says sarcastically.

"Somehow I don't think that's Jack's mess." Adam says.

"What do you…? Ahh."

"Jack. Jack, are you in? We need your help." Dylan shouts.

"It's starting to look more like he may need our help."

Dylan makes his way up the stairs.

"Jack are you in? Are you okay?"

He opens the bedroom door and puts on the light. He jumps back when he sees Jacks body lying on the bed.

"What? What is it?" Casey shouts trying to see past the other boys.

"Jack. Jack, wake up." Dylan shouts.

"Somehow I don't think Jack's sleeping." Casey says.

"Will you shut up?"

Dylan walks forward and touches his neck to feel for a pulse and knows straight away that he's dead.

"He's freezing and look at the marks on his neck."

"Well we can rule out Jack helping us then." Casey says.

Adam looks at Casey and shakes his head. He picks up a sheet and pulls it up to cover Jack's body.

"What do you think happened?" Naz says.

"Well he didn't strangle himself now did he?" Casey says.

"But why would...?" Naz stops in mid sentence as Adam puts his finger to his lips.

"Shhh, guys be quiet."

In the distance they could hear police sirens and they begin to get louder.

"Come on. We've got to get out of here."

The boys rush down the stairs and as they reach the front door they can see the blue flashing lights speeding up the street. The first police car screeches to a halt in front of Jack's house and the officers catch sight of the boys as they run around the side of the house. The officer in the passenger seat is quick off the mark and gives chase. As he runs after them he takes out his torch in one hand and his truncheon in the other. He catches up with the boys as they are midway through climbing the fence. The officer lifts up his arm holding the truncheon as he approaches Naz.

He brings it down hard on the top of his head which sends him crashing to the ground on the other side of the fence. He puts his truncheon back in his utility belt as he tries to climb the fence and Adam smacks him in the face with a shovel. It startles him but he doesn't hit the deck. Adam hits him again and he goes down. He drops the shovel and grabs hold of Naz's arm.

"Come on. Run."

Naz is dragged to his feet and pulled up the path by Adam. They are out of sight by the time the other officers arrive. Dylan grew up in this area and knows it like the back of his hand. He leads the way through many gardens and out onto the main road.

"We can't go on the main road Dylan, they'll be driving up here any minute." Stuart says.

"Look I know what I'm doing. Trust me. They'll have the dogs out, we'll have to shake off our scent."

He crosses the main road which takes them to two streets with rows of tenements. He orders them to split up and run through the front of the tenements and out the back all the way along the street.

"If you see a wall, climb it. We'll meet at the other end." The boys do exactly as Dylan says and cross each others paths as they run which will help confuse the dogs. They carry on up the street and climb the large wall at the end.

"Right guys follow me." Dylan says.

"I don't think I can run anymore." Topher says lifting up his chest to help him take in more air to his lungs.

"It's okay it's not far."

"Why are you so unfit Topher? Is that because you used to smoke?" Naz asks.

"I never smoked. I only said that when I got caught with a lighter or matches. They were only for setting things on fire."

Dylan runs across the main road towards the base of Law Hill, a large hill which is located in the centre of the city. The base is surrounded by thick woodland and from the housing area at the bottom there is a road that winds through the trees until it reaches its summit, 174 metres above sea level. This attracts the tourists as they can view the whole city and beyond from each angle. At night though, the place is in total darkness, but Dylan knows exactly where he is going. He has been through here many times in the dark when he ran away as a young boy. The rest of the boys follow him as they are guided by a small light coming through the trees from the moonlit night sky. Dylan eventually comes to a large wire fence that surrounds an area of allotments. He is about to climb the fence but the place he wants to get to is at the other side and he realises the amount of footprints they would leave. He walks around to the other side of the allotments and climbs over the fence. He waits on the others and then walks over to a small shed. He puts his hand under the gap in the door.

"It's been a long time. My hands are nearly too big to fit through the gap."

He slides out the key and unlocks the door.

"Whose place is this?" Stuart asks.

"It's an old guy who lives near here. He knew the trouble I was in at home and said if needed some place to go…well I guess he still leaves the key for me."

11.

A full scale search for the boys went on through the night until the early hours of the morning. Officers from other areas were drafted in to help with the door to door enquiries. The police began to think that the boys were hiding in one of the tenement flat as this was where the dogs began to lose the scent.

  Smith was tired but decided to go back to his office before going home for some much needed sleep. He had a message on his desk that Jack's time of death was approximately two in the afternoon. Surely the boys wouldn't have hung around all that time. The call to the police station to inform them about the murder was from a woman and was made from a phone box five miles away. Something didn't add up. Whoever made that call had to have been there to know Jack was already dead. If she saw the boys kill him why did she go five miles away to make the call. Smith was starting to stress himself out going over the events in his head trying to piece it altogether. He began to prepare a statement for the press when a folder that had recently been placed on his desk attracted his attention. It was nearly an inch thick and had a post-it attached.

F.A.O.
D.C.I. Smith
As he opened the folder he was faced with photos of all six boys. It was their files and background reports. He flicked

through each of them and one photo stood out more than the others. Adam. Looking at the photo he thought he knew him from somewhere. He started to read it in more detail. *'Taken into care at the age of four after both parents were killed in a car crash...father - William McGinty...brother William McGinty...'*

"William...its Billy's baby brother." He mumbles to himself.

Smith sits back in his chair but keeps his eyes focused on the folder lying open in front of him. He stares at the photo of Adam and can now see the resemblance to Billy and his father. He begins to think about the past when he was still a struggling detective.

The McGinty's had just arrived in Dundee. Billy, his pregnant wife and their young son, also called Billy, had come over from the province of Northern Ireland to escape the troubles. Billy senior had just come out of The Maze also known as Long Kesh prison after a long stretch. In the time he was inside he had witnessed many of his friends lose some of their close relatives. Upon his release he looked on as his own son had become more and more involved in the troubles. He had tried to guide him away from it but like everyone else it was in their faces everyday and it was hard to ignore it. He was worried for his son and knew that one day he would end up going to prison like himself or worse, he would end up dead. When his wife announced she was pregnant again he knew he had to move away.

Not long after arriving in Dundee, Billy's wife gave birth to another son, Adam, and it was around this time that Smith first came across young Billy. He had found it hard to settle after knowing only violence and crime his whole life. One night as Smith was given the task of taking young Billy back home after having been picked up for a minor crime, he was taken aback by the hostility he received from the boy and his father and the hatred they had for the police. It had come to the point where officers avoided arresting young Billy so as they did not have to face his father. Each time young Billy was mentioned between officers he was known as Billy's kid. After several appearances at the children's panel Billy's parents were informed that there were only so many excuses they could make for young Billy and the next time he appeared they would be considering the possibility of putting him into Borstal. This news must have given young Billy a scare as he began to settle down and avoided getting himself into trouble for a long time. Billy's parents occasionally travelled back to Ireland to visit relatives and with Billy's progress they thought it best that he stayed here. They did not want him to be mixing with his old friends and reverting back to his old ways.

It was during one of their parent's visits back home, while Adam was being looked after by family friends Old Charlie and Kathy, that Billy received the phone call. It was the devastating news that they had been killed in a car crash. Charlie and Kathy stuck by young Billy and travelled back with him to bury his parents. They were granted custody of Adam and asked young Billy to come back with them as this is what his parents would have wanted. Billy felt as though he had nothing and soon reverted back to his old ways of violence and crime. Only this time Billy was no longer a minor and his crimes were becoming more serious. He had grown wise to the authorities and they were finding it harder to catch him. He had a close circle of friends that were loyal and like any organisation, it had a leader, Billy. Billy was becoming known, he was no longer Billy's kid, and was now being referred to as Billy the kid. The police had little evidence but they knew Billy and his friends were behind several robberies that had occurred in the city. Smith, who was put in charge of the case, had picked up one of Billy's circle of friends. One who liked to talk. Every move Billy made, Smith was onto him. The police were closing in and Billy knew it was only a matter of time before he was caught. He made a decision, he had to leave.

Smith looked over at the press statement that he had started to write and suddenly an idea comes into his head. He has had his doubts about the boys killing Jay from the start and he should be out following up leads but he has waited for an opportunity like this for a long, long time. This situation could give him the chance to catch Billy's kid. He now feels wide awake and pulls his chair closer to his desk. He rips up the original statement and starts again.

***

The boys had been hiding out in the shed for two days now. Dylan had left early each morning with Stuart and brought back rolls, milk and newspapers for the rest of the boys. They had watched, from the top of the Law, the deliveries being made and quickly swooped down to help themselves. On the third morning Adam had watched through a small window in the roof of the shed and had noticed that the night sky was starting to clear. He had lain awake for hours and like the other boys, he had become restless. He nudged Dylan who was sound asleep and snoring away. Dylan was reluctant to move until Adam mentioned that if they didn't go for food now they would have to wait until tomorrow. Dylan was soon on his feet, stretching and ready to go. They walked to the top of the Law and looked down on the empty streets below. They could see the top of the police incident box at the end of Jack's street. No doubt containing some bored officers being paid to sit in there and drink coffee all night.

They watch the same milk float as yesterday doing its deliveries and Adam stands up. "Not this one." Dylan says shaking his head.

"Why not?"

"We done that one yesterday."

"So?"

"If it's a one off they won't notice but if their deliveries are short two days in a row they'll know someone's at it."

"I take it you've done this a lot?"

Dylan doesn't answer but gives him a smile
They don't have to wait long before they see another milk float in another area to the left of them. They walk slowly down the hill to the streets below and casually walk to a local shop and help themselves to rolls and newspapers that have been delivered less than an hour before. On the way back up the hill they take a detour to the area where the milk had been delivered and take cartons of milk from random doorsteps before heading back to the shed.

Topher was the first to open up one of the newspapers as he munched on a roll.

"Adam."

"Yeah, what is it?"

"I think you had better take a look at this."

Topher turns the paper around and the rest of the boys squeeze together to read under the small light from the roof window. The story was a double page spread about Adam's brother with a large photo of him from when he was younger.

"He looks just like you Adam." Casey says.

"Why? What does it say?" Naz says.

"Oh I forgot, do you need it translated?" Casey says.

"No I just can't see for your big head."

Adam looks up and stares at them and they both go quiet and put their heads down.

"It says here that Adam's brother Billy is still wanted in connection with a few armed robberies from over ten years ago." Dylan says.

"What else?" Naz says.

Dylan scans down the page.

"Billy's brother Adam is the leader of the gang of runaways who are now wanted in connection with two murders…that means they think we killed Jack as well."

"Gang, they think we're a gang now, and Adam's our leader." Casey says.

"Yeah but look at the photo of Adam."

"That's me?" Stuart says.

Adam takes the paper and sits staring at the photo of his brother and Stuart as he reads the article over again. He thinks about what his brother must have been like back then and tries to imagine what he would do in this situation.

"Guys, seriously I think we should hand ourselves in now. This has got way out of hand." Stuart pleads.

"I'm not handing myself in. I've done nothing wrong." Naz says

"All the more reason for us to go back and tell them it wasn't us. We wouldn't be in this situation if it wasn't for you." Stuart says looking angrily at Adam.

"What's that supposed to mean?" Adam says looking up from the paper.

"Well it was your idea to go to Jack's house. If we hadn't

gone there we wouldn't have got caught coming out of his house and we wouldn't be in this situation."

Adam snaps back. "So it's all my fault then is it? I guess it's my fault for walking in on Frank and Bruce when they had Jay tied to his chair while they beat him to death."

"Are you sure it wasn't you that done it? And maybe they walked in on you."

Adam dives over and smashes Stuart with his fist in the side of the face. Stuart's head goes back and they both end up rolling around on the floor. Adam manages to get on top and throws punch after punch to Stuart's head.

Dylan pulls Adam off and the rest of the boys keep Stuart back.

"You're just as much to blame for this as me. I never asked you to come here. I never asked you to come to Jack's house either. If you want to go and hand yourself in then off you go. None of us will stop you. Just remember, to them, your hands are just as dirty as mine." Adam shouts.

"Guys. Guys." Naz says as he tries to get both their attention.

"Look no-one here is to blame; we're all in this together."

Adam and Stuart sit back and nothing is said between the two. The rest of the boys also sit in silence as they contemplate their options. As Adam passes the paper on to Naz, who has been waiting patiently to read the story, he thinks of a plan but knows it's not the right time to bring it up. He decides to keep quiet and see how things turn out.

***

Smith had been in the office all morning looking over the notes from all the various vague sightings of the boys from the past two days. He picks up his jacket, as he is about to go out for lunch. D.C. Nevin appears with a large map in her hand. She spreads it across his desk. Three areas are circled in pencil. Smith recognises one of the areas as Jack's street.

"What are these?" he says pointing to the two other circles.

"We've received a report from a shop in the glens area. There was a quantity of rolls stolen early this morning and residents have complained about their milk not being delivered when the dairy was adamant that they delivered it. The two detectives stand and stare at the map laid out in front of them. Dylan had specifically chosen to steal from different areas so as not to alert suspicion but Nevin was looking at it in exactly the same way. She tried to place herself in certain locations where the boys could be hiding and would be able to obtain access to all of these areas. She mentioned to Smith the different locations and put together scenarios of why the boys would be in these particular places. Smith stood and stared at the map for a long time.

"I think we are looking too much at the bigger picture."

"What do you mean?"

"Well if I send out teams of officers to all these locations that you mention it will use up all our resources. If the boys see the large police presence they will be less likely to come out of hiding or it could even make them move further away. I believe they are a lot closer than we think. Another day won't hurt so wait until tomorrow, if more deliveries go missing we could narrow the area down further. Have extra officers on stand-by for tomorrow morning and as soon as the report comes in we'll move."

Nevin picks up the map and walks out of the office. Smith follows her as far as the stair landing and then turns towards the lift. He knows if this works out the boys or at least some of the boys will be in custody by this time tomorrow. This is not what he has planned but he knows he has to appear genuine enough about catching the boys. If any of his superiors knew his intentions he would be sacked on the spot.

***

Billy had been hard at work sanding the crumbling paint from the underside of a small boat when he felt a tap on his shoulder. It was Nina, Billy's girlfriend of several years. When Billy left Scotland he travelled around for a long time working various jobs to pay his way. He had met Nina in a bar one night and she mentioned that her grandfather was looking for a hand cleaning up old boats on the beach. He died a couple of years ago but Billy had learned enough from him to manage the place on his own. Nina deals with all the business side of things.

"Yeah, what is it?" He says as he lifts up his dust mask.

"You have a phone call."

"Who is it?"

"I don't know. I couldn't really understand him he talked very fast. He asked for Billy the kid."

Billy smiles upon hearing this as he knows the only person from back home who has his number is his old friend Kevin.

"Hello."

"Is this Billy's kid?" He asks, trying to put on a posh voice.

"How's it going Kev. What's up? Let me guess, you've

heard some gossip that you just have to tell someone."

"Nah nah, nothing like that, I just wondered if you get our newspapers out there"

"Yeah, they're usually a day or two late but yeah. Why?"

"Do you know about the gang of youngsters from Dundee who are on the run? They're suspected of murder" Billy is about to answer a question with a question but feels he already knows the answer.

"Adam." he blurts out.

"Yeah. They've been on the run for a few days now and this morning every national newspaper has your picture in it."

"My picture?"

"Don't worry it's one from when you were about sixteen. It has a photo with Adam's name next to it but I don't think it's him."

"What's the story? What's it all about?"

"Just a group of kids from a boys home that apparently killed the guy who was running the place and then two days ago a warden who worked there was found dead in his house. I never really paid much attention to it until your picture appeared. Look I'll put the word out and get back to you when I find out more about it."

"Okay be quick."

"No probs mate."

"Bye."

Billy puts the receiver down and stares at the wall.

"What wrong Billy." Nina says. Sensing it's bad news.

"It's my kid brother. He's in a lot of trouble. I think I'll have to go back and help him."

"I thought you said you could never go back."

"I can't, but if my brother needs my help…Nina could you try and get hold of some British newspapers, the later the edition, the better."

"Where are you going?"

"I'll have to go use up a few favours that I'm due."

12.

It was the third night that the boys had stayed in the shed. This didn't appear to bother Dylan too much as he had stayed here for a week, sometimes longer, on his own but the rest of the boys were starting to get restless. There was the constant feeling of hunger and this resulted in petty arguments that escalated to Dylan having to step in before they came to blows. None of the boys had slept on that third night and it was still dark when he announced that he was going for a walk up the hill. The other boys decided to go with him. As they sat at the top of the Law looking down on the whole of the city below the sky started to became clearer. Topher comments on the deliveries being made to a shop down below.

"That shop is only one street away from Jack's house." Dylan says.

"So?"

"So do you see that white box lit up down there? That's full of police waiting to catch us."

"Exactly that's the last place they would expect us to go." Topher says.

There is silence for a few seconds as the boys look down below.

"He's right you know." Adam says.

The boys all look at each other.

"Come on, let's go. My stomach has been rumbling all night." Dylan says as he gets up and starts walking down the hill.

When they reach the bottom the boys split up. Dylan, Stuart and Naz go to the shop to steal the rolls and Adam, Casey and Topher go in search of milk. On approaching the street with the police incident box Casey notices cartons of milk on the doorsteps opposite.

"Topher." He says nudging him and nodding in the direction of the milk.

Topher smiles back and then swaggers out from the bushes where they are hiding.

"Don't be stupid." Adam says in a loud whisper.

Topher looks back with a large grin as his swagger is exaggerated upon reaching the police box. He walks past and straight to the garden opposite. He picks up two cartons of milk and casually walks back to the bushes.

"You're not right mate." Casey says and laughs.

As the boys walk back to meet the others at the bottom of the Law they walk through more side streets and pick up some more cartons of milk. Casey also manages to take some newspapers back out of their letter boxes.

They make their way back up the Law and sit stuffing their faces with the freshly made rolls. Casey opens one of the newspapers and nudges Stuart.

"What is it?"

Casey nods at the story in the paper and both boys look at each other.

"Dylan."

"Yeah. What is it?"

Neither boy says a word but stare back at Dylan. He looks at the page and takes the paper from Casey. Dylan's smile soon drops from his face as he looks on in disgust at a photo of his father in a wheelchair with his mother by his side. Above the photo is the heading 'This is what my son, the killer, did to me.' The story goes on to say how Dylan used to beat up his father on a regular basis and one day he went too far. Now his father needs twenty four hour care.

Dylan sits down and reads the full story then looks up to see all the boys crowded around him. He knows that even if the story was true none of these boys would ever judge him. They all have a past and they were all picked by Jay for the same reason. Although feeling hurt and angry, Dylan looks at the other boys and smiles. He now realises the extent in which Jays influence has had on them. He looks back at the newspaper and one thing that stands out to him is the part of the heading that says 'Killer.' This gives Dylan a bit of a reality check.

"Guys they've called me a killer."

Adam laughs "I wouldn't take it personally Dylan."

"No, but you don't understand. Some people WILL believe it."

"Dylan we're all in this together mate." Casey says.

Dylan throws the paper aside and watches as it soaks up the wet from the ground.

"Good one Dylan. How are the rest of us supposed to read it now." Naz says.

"What do you mean? You can't read anyway." Casey says.

"Guys I think we should get back to the shed before we're seen." Stuart says.

"Is there no where else we can go to hide out, I really don't want to be stuck in there all day again." Topher says.

Dylan walks off in the direction of the shed and the boys follow with Casey and Naz trying to trip each other up as they walk.

"Shh." Adam says as he stops suddenly.

"What is it?" Dylan whispers.

"Look over there." he says pointing through the trees.

The boys look to see several police officers with torches at the foot of the Law. Casey is too interested in tripping up Naz to notice what's going on and laughs out loud when Naz goes head first down a small mud slide. The rest of the boys give Casey a stern look. They watch as the torches begin moving in their direction. For all the abuse Casey gives Naz he is the first one down the hill to help him. The boys move quickly through the trees but Adam doesn't know where he is going and leads them to the base of the Law, stopping short of the road.

"Where do we go now Dylan?"

Dylan makes a quick decision. He knows it will lead to more trouble but after reading the lies in the newspaper only minutes before he decides to go for it.

"Follow me." He says.

Dylan runs across the main road and climbs a fence into someone's back garden. He keeps on running until he reaches his destination. He opens the back door to a tenement block and waits inside for the others to catch up.

"Where are we?" Adam asks as he struggles for breath.

Dylan doesn't answer but nods to a door behind him. Adam reads the name plate on the door. 'McKay'

"Are you sure this is a good idea?"

Dylan shrugs his shoulders. "Where else are we going to go?"

"What are we waiting here for?" Casey asks.

They all look at Dylan for an answer. He looks at the door and hesitates for a few seconds. He signals for the others to stand away from the door out of sight. With his stomach in knots he knocks on the door lightly. No answer. He clatters the letter box and waits anxiously.

"Who is it?" A voice behind the door says.

"It's Tayside Police." He says in a deep voice.

His mother opens the door and before he looks at her a familiar smell wafts from inside the house. The rancid smell of dirty smoke and stale alcohol. Dylan's mother stares at him for a few seconds before she recognises who he is. He has grown in height and filled out considerably. After years of malnutrition he is now a muscular and clean cut young man. Although sleeping rough the past week hasn't helped much.

"Dylan. What are you doing here?" She says sounding distraught.

"Yeah it's good to see you too mum." He says sarcastically.

"What do you want?"

"Me and my friends need a place to hang out for a bit."

"So you come crawling back here after everything you've put us through."

"I knew this was a bad idea." Dylan mumbles as he goes to walk away.

He looks at the other boys faces. Tired, dirty and cold, he turns back again and pushes the door wide open.

"Mum these are my friends and we're going to be staying for a while." He says pushing past his mother and marching through the house.

The other boys trail behind him with their heads down as they walk past Dylan's mother. Dylan opens the living room door and the foul smell really hits him. The dark room is littered with empty tins and bottles. Dylan's father sits in a drunken stupor in his wheelchair in front of the television. His mother was obviously too drunk last night to put him to his bed. The boys look on from the doorway as Dylan clears the couch and chairs of rubbish.

"Grab a seat guys. I'll go and put the kettle on."

Dylan walks into the kitchen to find his mother pouring herself a drink.

"Now, there's a familiar scene."

He opens the fridge to find a full crate of cheap lager and takes them out.

"What are you doing with them. They're your uncle Jimmy's."

"Where is he?"

"He's sleeping in your old room."

Dylan smiles.

"How convenient. Well, I'm sure he won't mind."

Dylan feared his uncle Jimmy as much as his father when he was growing up. As he had subjected him to as much, if not more, physical abuse than his father had. Dylan walks into the living room where the boys have gathered around the television waiting patiently on the local morning news.

"Help yourselves guys."

The boys' eyes light up at the thought of being offered alcohol. They all lean forward and take a tin, all except Naz.

"Is that beer? I don't drink beer?" Naz says.

"Get it down you, you wimp." Casey says.

Naz feels the peer pressure and reluctantly opens a tin and sips from it.

"That's disgusting."

The boys all laugh.

"Just keep drinking. You'll get used to it. The first taste is always like that." Topher says.

"Yeah and before you know it, you'll be living in a hole like this and be drinking the stuff for breakfast," Dylan says.

He shouts on his mother who is busy in the kitchen topping up her drink. He tells her to make up some food. His father begins to stir from his slumber and realising his son is in the house he shouts on Dylan's mother to call the police. Dylan sits in front of him laughing.

"You don't have a phone."

"Why are you here? Don't you think you've caused enough trouble?"

"Shh. Guys here's the news." Topher says.

Dylan's father is still ranting and raving so Dylan slaps him in the head.

"Shut it, or I'll give you something to shout about."

The boys look on in shock, as they have never seen Dylan act like that before. They all look back at the screen as the report tells a complete fictional story of what happened. It goes onto say that the gang of boys, are suspected of torturing and killing their mentor Jason Fallon and only several days ago they were seen fleeing from the house where a security warden from the program was found strangled. The gang is believed to be led by teenager Adam McGinty. At this point on the TV they show a photo of Stuart and all the boys laugh.

"What the hell have you boys done?"

Dylan's mother shouts as she stands in the doorway holding two large plates of toast.

"Here. Let me help you with those Mrs McKay." Casey says as he takes the plate from her shaky hands. Before Casey gets the chance to sit back down several hands appear and the plates are soon empty as the boys attention is back at the screen.

"Tayside Police Detective Chief Inspector Smith released a statement saying that these boys are violent and dangerous and should not be approached under any circumstances. If any of the public sees any of these boys they should contact the police straight away."

Adam changes the channel.

"Where do we go from here?" Topher says.

"Ask our leader." Naz says.

"Which one?" Topher says looking at Adam then at Stuart continuously. The rest of the boys laugh, except Stuart who gives Adam a snide look. As the boys discuss their options Dylan's uncle Jimmy appears in the doorway.

"What the hell is going on here? Is that my beer?"

"No, that WAS your beer. Now it's ours." Dylan says.

"Oh, so now you think you're some sort of hard man coming back here with your little gang."

"There's no 'sort of' about it." Dylan says.

Jimmy steps forward to go for Dylan but Adam stands up blocking his path and squares up to him. Jimmy is a big man with rough scary looking features due to his chosen life of alcohol abuse.

He towers over Adam but looks relatively thin due to Adams broad shoulders.

Jimmy laughs. "And what do you think you're going to do?" he says gritting his teeth and screwing up his face. That look from Jimmy had made many hard men back down in the past. Dylan had also seen the expression many times and still cringes at the thought of what would usually come with it. Adam is unfazed as he too has seen this expression, only on different faces from many different bullies he has encountered in the past. Casey stands and walks to the side of Adam. Stuart looks at the others and they all stand up except Dylan who stays seated. He smiles at Jimmy. Jimmy looks around the room at these young boys' faces and sees, lurking behind those innocent wide staring eyes, a violence and hatred that are waiting to erupt. Although Jimmy has always acted tough throughout his life he knows his limits. Even through alcohol he knows how far he can go and when to walk away. This is one of those times. He turns on his heels and walks out of the living room and into the kitchen. He sees the bottle of vodka next to the sink and starts to pour himself a drink. Images start to flash into his head as he gulps down straight from the bottle. He starts to think about all the times that he abused his brother's kid. All the times he should have stepped in when his brother was beating this poor defenceless boy black and blue. When his brother got tired he would sometimes take over. He used to laugh when his brother took off his belt and used the buckle to whip him when his punches didn't appear to be having any effect. Every now and again the beatings were so extreme Dylan wouldn't be allowed out of the house until the wounds healed. The only reason Dylan did not tell anyone what was going on was that he was afraid if he was taken away his mother would receive the beatings instead.

Dylan walked through to the kitchen to see his uncle Jimmy crouched on the floor with the drink in his hand. Jimmy rose to his feet and stood inches from Dylan's face. He could smell the alcohol from his breath. Looking straight into his eyes he wondered to himself why his own uncle hated him so much. He was now past caring. Dylan titled his head back slightly and launched forward hitting his forehead on the bridge of Jimmy's nose. Jimmy crumbled to the floor. He looked up to see Dylan standing over him with the same look and gritted teeth that he had shown him only moments before. Jimmy started to feel sorry for himself and Dylan saw tears running down his cheek.

"Why are you crying? It's only wimps that cry. Do you remember you used to say that to me? Do you remember you used to tell my father to hit me harder if I cried? It will toughen him up you used to say. Well it toughened me up alright. Tough enough to take a beating from both of you and still walk away. The only reason you are not in a wheelchair like that pathetic excuse I have for a father is because you weren't there that day. The day I realised why I was taking those beatings. It was to stop my mother from taking them, the same mother who did nothing to stop me from getting those beatings in the first place. The same mother I caught in bed with you."

Jimmy looks up through his tears.

"Oh did I forget to mention that before. Look at you, you're pathetic. Sitting there feeling sorry for yourself." Dylan turns to walk away and sees all his friends standing in the doorway.

"How long have you guys been stand…"

"DYLAN." Adam shouts.

Dylan turns to see Jimmy with a bread knife in his hand. He lunges forward and Dylan uses his arm to block it. The blade slices through his arm but Dylan manages to grab Jimmy's wrist. There is a struggle as they go from one side of the kitchen to the other. Dylan manages to turn Jimmy's wrist away from him so that the blade is facing outwards, Jimmy is shouting that he's going to kill him. Adam steps forward to try and help but the pair stumble back and Jimmy trips over Adams foot. They both fall to the floor. Dylan gets up quickly, grabs a towel and wraps it around his arm. He looks over at the other boys who are staring down at the floor behind him. He looks around to see Jimmy's body lying motionless on his back with the knife sticking out of his stomach.

They all stand in shock as Dylan's mother squeezes past and screams.

"Get her out of here." Dylan says.

Casey puts his arms around her shoulders and takes her back to the living room.

"Is he dead?" Topher asks.

"Feel free to check." Adam says gesturing to Topher with his hand.

"Nah, I think he's dead." He says satisfied with his observation.

"What are we going to do now?" Naz asks but no-one answers.

Adam marches past everyone and into the bedroom were he takes the quilt off the bed. He walks back into the kitchen and places it over Jimmy's body.

Stuart helps Dylan clean up the blood from his arm. He rips up a dish towel and wraps it around tightly to stop the blood flow.

"You really need some stitches in that."

"Well I can't exactly turn up at the hospital can I?"

"Come on you guys let's go next door." Adam says ushering everyone to the living room.

Naz walks in first and picks up a tin of beer and opens it.

"How does it taste now?" Casey asks.

"Quite good actually"

Dylan picks one up next.

"Well I guess he won't need them now."

"How dare you. You're evil. You've just killed him and now you think it's funny." Dylan's mother says.

"He tried to kill me. I wasn't the one who picked up the knife, he was. So shut you're trap. Anyway he had it coming."

Dylan's mother leaps from her seat and starts laying into him with punches and kicks. He grabs her and throws her across the room.

"It should have been you lying next door, not Jimmy." he shouts.

"Why? So that you can carry on sleeping with him?" Dylan's father turns his head swiftly to look at his mother.

"Oh did you not know." Dylan says with a smug grin on his face.

Dylan's father looks at him. The boys sit in silence drinking their tins of beer. They stare at the television and occasionally glance at each other trying to blank out the drama going on next to them.

"I think its time for us to move on." Stuart says but nobody moves.

"Where are we going to go? The police will be all over the place by now." Casey says.

"Why don't you take your friends to your lying little girlfriend's house? Oh, but her father moved to keep you away from her. What is she going to think of you now? You're murderers, the lot of you." She shouts as she looks around at the other boys.

Dylan catches Adam's eye and nods towards the door.

"Right guys, time to go" Adam says and the rest of the boys stand up. Much to the annoyance of Stuart.

"Where are we going?" Casey says.

Adam shrugs his shoulders and walks towards the door. The rest of the boys follow. Naz picks up the rest of the tins of beer.

"I thought you said it was disgusting." Topher says.

Naz smiles back through a now drunken gaze.

On the way towards the front door the boys have to walk past the kitchen and each of them look at the now blood soaked quilt covering Jimmy's body and then quickly look away.

Once outside the boys realise they are running out of

places to go. It's still early morning and the streets are beginning to get busy with people travelling to work. Stuart takes charge and announces he is going to Rich's flat.

"He's our last hope of getting help to prove that we didn't kill Jay."

The rest of the boys nod in agreement. Accept Adam, who silently has other ideas about the whole situation.

13.

Councillor Williamson had several interviews set up throughout the day. The situation had gone way beyond what he could have ever imagined. As he lay in bed in the early hours of the morning he began to plan his speech. The local newspaper had contacted him but none of the nationals. They were only interested in the gory details and the background of each of the boys. His phone rang. It was Frank.

"Councillor. They're on the news. The police discovered their hideout but they managed to escape again."
The councillor didn't even say goodbye. He put the phone down and got out of bed. He went downstairs where his wife was already cooking his breakfast. His usual greasy fry up did not appeal to him today. He wanted to get to his office as soon as possible.

On arrival at the office he could see Frank waiting outside with his latest employee, Rich. The councillor took several deep breaths as he approached them and barely noticed Heather's desk as he walked past. It had been covered in small post it notes from people trying to get in touch with her over the past few days. The councillor stepped into his office and Frank and Rich followed. He took off his suit jacket to reveal his massive frame and turned to face them with his large fake grin as he prepared himself. He tried to sound as genuine and concerned as possible as this would be a dry run for the cameras later on in the day. He offered the boy tea or coffee and put a large plate of his tempting gold foil wrapped biscuits in front of him. Frank's hand was hovering over the plate even before it was put down. Frank rarely ever saw this side of Williamson. It was usually only the angry threatening side to him he saw. He knew it was all a show for the boy's sake but he also knew what was coming.

He was drawing him in before getting what he wanted and then he would find a way to get rid of him.

Rich though, wasn't stupid, he was intelligent enough to know when he was being played. Rich had a tough background. The abusive father. The life of crime. He was tough and even on the program when Frank and Bruce started on him he was never intimidated. He once stood toe to toe with them and warned each of them that as soon as he left the program he would come looking for them. But somewhere along the line he changed and was soon bought over by his new boss, a man he did have a genuine fear of. It wasn't the fact that Williamson was well over six foot and towered over Rich by several inches. Nor was it his fearsome reputation as Rich never knew anything about him. It was actually the way he made everyone else feel in his presence. Frank who was not much smaller than Williamson would squirm in his seat and answer him as if he was being interrogated. Frank always looked scared in Williamson's company and this is what made Rich wary of him. After all the small talk was out of the way Williamson went to work on Rich by asking him about the other boys. Where would they be most likely to hide out. Had he seen them or had they contacted him. Rich's answers appeared to be not enough to convince Williamson that he was telling the truth and he began to get impatient. He slowly paced his office floor talking about The Program and how much he respected Jay and wanted to help the boys before they got into anymore trouble. He walked behind the large comfortable chairs where Frank and Rich were sitting and with one large swoop he threw his arm around Rich and grabbed him by the throat, picking him out of the chair. He dragged him backwards and pinned him against the wall.

"Tell me where they are?" He shouted.

Rich starts to choke and tries his hardest to pull Williamson's hands away but he is too strong. Williamson grips tighter and Rich struggles for breath.

"Councillor" Frank shouts.

Williamson looks at Frank and back to Rich who is seconds from passing out. He releases his grip from Rich's throat but uses the other hand to grab his groin.

"Where are they?" He shouts.

"I don't know. I haven't seen them." Rich coughs and splutters.

Williamson lets him go and casually walks away to his seat behind his desk. He gestures for both of them to sit down again. Williamson takes out a thick envelope from his drawer, smiles at Rich and throws it on his desk.

"It's yours. Take it."

"What is it?"

"It's a, a working bonus if you like. Here take it." He says picking it up and handing it over to him. Rich looks at Frank who nods at him to encourage him to take it. As he leans forward and grips the envelope Williamson grabs his wrist and leaps up out of his seat. His face is screwed up and is inches from Rich's.

"Now you take that envelope and you make sure you treat yourself well with what's in it. And if these friends of yours come knocking on your door. You be sure to tell Frank here."

"He let go his wrist and his face drops to his fake smile again.

"Now off you go and wait outside while I go over some things with Frank."

As soon as Rich is out of the office Williamson stares at Frank. He points his finger at him as if he is talking to a child.

"If you ever butt in again when I'm questioning someone it will be the biggest mistake you ever make.

Now go and drive him home and make sure he understands the situation."

Frank walks out of the office and Williamson sits back in his chair with his smug grin.

As Rich was being driven home by Frank he started to feel sick.

"Stop the car."

Rich opens the door and pukes up at the side of the road. He closes the door and looks down at the envelope in his hand. He has just been bought and Frank knows how he feels as he was once in the same position many years ago.

"Don't worry it will pass."

"Excuse me."

"The guilty feeling; It will pass."

Rich looks on in disgust. They arrive at Rich's block of flats and as he opens the car door Frank grabs his arm.

"Look, you don't have to get involved. If your friends get in touch just let us know."

Rich pulls his arm free and gives Frank a stare before slamming the door shut. He runs up the stairs of his building but before he reaches his door he stops. He looks at the envelope and tears it open. His eyes widen. It is a bundle of fifty pound notes. He has never even seen one of these before and now he has an envelope full of them.

He hurries to his door and fumbles around with his key due to his excitement. Once inside he goes to the kitchen and starts to count it. He finds a place to hide it under his sink and sits down. Seconds later he pulls it back out and looks at it. He smiles from ear to ear then begins counting it again.

***

Billy had worked hard over the last few days to finish off some of the smaller jobs. It was the morning of his departure back to Scotland and he was unsure of what lay ahead. He was about to travel by cargo ship back to Liverpool docks and from there he would travel by train to Edinburgh where his friend would pick him up and drive him the rest of the way to Dundee. He phoned his old friend Kevin to make sure that his arrival would be away from preying eyes. He was reassured he would be safe but was also informed of the news of the latest murder, apparently by the boys. Before Billy boarded the ship he said his goodbye to a tearful Nina and promised her he would be back.

***

Councillor Williamson marched towards his office after his extra long lunch break. The receptionist walked by his side informing him of his messages. He stepped into his office and closed the door as she was in mid sentence.
"Fat arrogant pig." she muttered to herself.
The councillor sat down at his desk which was covered in small yellow post-it notes with names and numbers. He scanned through them quickly but none of them appeared

to be important enough for him to call back straight away. He was hoping some of them would be from the national newspapers or television stations wanting an interview on the now triple murder spree.

"Councillor that's D.C.I Smith for you." The receptionist announces through the intercom.

"Tell him I'm busy. I'll call him back."

"No I mean he's here, outside your office."

The councillor feels a sudden embarrassment in knowing that he must have heard this. He'll have her fired within the week, he thinks to himself, as he opens his office door and extends his arm to shake the Detectives hand.

"Come in to my office. Have a seat. Would you like some tea or coffee?"

"Coffee would be good thanks." Smith says.

"Mary, could you bring in a tray of refreshments please."

This was one of the perks Smith liked about his job. Wherever he went he was always offered tea or coffee. After the introductions were out of the way Mary appears with the coffee and the usual tray of biscuits. Smith sometimes wondered why council officials and business men were mostly all large fat people. Being served these treats at every opportunity is probably a major contribution.

Smith had known of the councillor's reputation and how ruthless he could be in a Board room. He had heard people talk in the past, saying that was one of the main reasons he was elected, for his no-nonsense, straight to the point attitude. He was well respected in the business world for his honesty and people thought he would come in and give the place a good shake up. Get out all the 'old wood' and stop all the 'jobs for the boys' they would say. The talk now is that he is ruthless alright, but only when he is lining his own pockets. If decisions don't go in his favour, pity anyone who is standing in his way.

As Smith and his partner sit in the large leather comfortable chairs facing Williamson. They look around his office taking in the fine décor and the marble floors. The best that tax payers' money can buy.

"So how can I help you?" The councillor says in his best suave tone that Smith can see through a mile off.

"We are investigating the murder of Jason Fallon and Jack Pearson."

"Tragic, tragic. I heard there was another murder this morning I hope you catch those boys soon detective."

"Yes well, I heard you are a man who likes to get straight to the point so if you wouldn't mind answering a few questions to help with our enquiries."

"Sure, go ahead."

"You had three staff working on the program from your department."

"Yes that's right. Frank, Bruce and Jack"

"Can you tell me why staff from your department were employed on the program."

"It's all to do with funding. You see the program was only granted so much money per year.

So when some departments have a larger budget they require we move some staff around to accommodate them."

Smith knows full well why his staff were on the program although proving it is another matter.

"Do you have an employee named Heather Low?"

"Yes. She's been off for a few days now." Williamson looks at the two Detectives confused as to why they would be enquiring about his assistant.

"Do you know she's Jacks sister?" Smith says not lifting his head from his notes. Smith has had all these questions planned in advance and his partner is studying the councillor's reaction to each one. Williamson has a look of shock and his mind is working overtime as to how much his, soon to be ex-assistant, knows and the real reason she hasn't turned up for work.

"We've been trying to contact her since the night of her brother's murder and she appears to have vanished. We can't trace her or her car."

Williamson shrugs his shoulders. For once he is struggling for an answer.

"I'm sorry but I haven't heard from her. She hasn't even phoned to explain why she is off."

Smith looks down his page of notes again and skips a few. He was bored of this. It was time for the big one.

"Do you know anything about a complaints book?"

"Sorry. A what?"

"You know, a note book. It was kept by Jason Fallon in his office and it apparently contained a list of complaints."

"Complaints about what exactly?"

"Your staff"

"I'm sorry, but this is news to me."

"Uh huh?" Smith says lifting his head from his notes and looking him straight in the eyes.

"Excuse me Detective but I don't like your tone. Are you accusing me of something?"

Williamson says quite aggressively.

"No, not at all. I'm simply asking if you have any knowledge of the whereabouts of the complaints book."

"No. I don't and any accusations towards my staff I take very seriously."

"So do we councillor. I think that will be all for now. I'm sure we'll be in touch."

Williamson sits back in his chair with his hands clasped

tightly together as he watches the detectives leave. He leans forward, picks up the receiver and dials a number.

"Frank"

"Yeah"

"We need to talk. Come up to my office as soon as possible."

He hangs up the receiver and sits back in his chair again as he considers his next move.

14.

After leaving Dylan's parents house the boys realise that they are running out of places to hide. The weather has turned cold and every corner they turn they have to hide quickly as slow moving patrol cars with eager police officers are looking to capture them. Hunger was beginning to be a problem again and this was resulting in the boys arguing. Stuart was still trying to show his authority over the other boys by urging them to go to Rich's. To his disappointment they all sided with Adam saying they thought that it was a bad idea. Dylan had not said a word since leaving his parents house and Adam had overheard Topher ask if he was okay which was returned with a grunt. The boys walked for several miles through back streets and waste ground to avoid being seen. They heard police sirens in the distance and when the sound appeared to be coming closer to them the boys froze, thinking they had been sighted. After coming across a derelict building they made the decision that they should hide out there until dark. The building was adjacent to an industrial estate. Half the windows were boarded up and the others were smashed with some of the window frames taken out. The boys climbed through one of the frameless holes and into what used to be a small factory. There were pieces of old machinery strewn across the floor with anything of value taken long ago. There were several doors located at the rear of the building and upon closer inspection Casey announced that one of these was a toilet after nearly retching at the smell as he opened the door. Stuart walked into a small room that was dimly lit from small holes in the board covering the window. The floor was carpeted and in the middle of the room was a desk and some broken chairs scattered around. After walking all morning in the cold and rain the small office felt warm to the boys. Dylan didn't say a word but found a space on the floor. He chose the dark corner and curled up with his back against the wall and his knees up close to his chest. The other boys followed and hardly a word was said between them as they closed their eyes. Although some of the boys managed to fall asleep it did not last as they would jerk themselves awake at the slightest noise. By early evening the small light they had coming in through the window had disappeared. The six boys sat in silence in the darkness shivering and hungry.

"So what's our next move Stuart?" Casey says.

"I think we should go to Rich's."

"That's what they'll expect us to do. They'll have someone watching him and no doubt he'll have been pulled in anyway and warned that if we contact him and he helps us then he'll be charged along with us." Adam says.

"I don't care. We can't keep going like this. At least at Rich's we would get some food and heat."

To the rest of the boys, hearing the words 'food' and 'heat' rang like a bell in their heads.

"If we go to Rich's we'll be caught for sure. I think this is a bad idea guys." Adam pleads.

"Well what do you suggest we do? Come on you seem to always have all the answers." Stuart snaps.

Adam can sense the rest of the boys looking at him even though he can't see any of their faces. He doesn't answer. Stuart stands up and feels his way along the wall until he reaches the door. As he opens it there is enough light from the street lights shining through for him to find his way out of the building.

The rain has stopped but the temperature has dropped some more.

"Which way do we go then Stuart?" Casey says.

"Don't look at me. I don't know where we are."

"Well then how are we supposed to get to Rich's?"

"I don't know I thought maybe one of you guys would know. Dylan?"

Dylan shrugs his shoulders. He knows exactly where Rich stays but he has other things on his mind at the moment and is not in the mood for talking.

"Oh great. Now we're lost. Whose stupid idea was it to come here anyway?" Casey asks.

The rest of the boys look at Stuart.

"It wasn't me." Stuart says.

"Why? You're the one that was out in front. We just assumed that you knew where you were going."
Casey says.
Adam looks on amused that the boys are now turning against Stuart.

"Wait a minute. If Dylan hadn't been so handy with that knife we maybe wouldn't have had to rush off so quickly." Stuart says.
The boys all look around at Dylan half expecting him to lunge at Stuart but he shrugs his shoulders and
wanders off.

"Good one Stuart." Adam says walking off to catch him up.

"Hold up mate. You okay."

"I need food." He says as he marches on faster.

"Dylan hold up. Look we're sorry about what happened

with you're uncle. We were all there, we know it wasn't your fault."

"I don't care about him. I don't care about any of my family."

"Well what's wrong?"

"I need to find somebody."

"Who?"

"A friend, I need to find her and let her know the truth."

"The girl you're mother mentioned."

"Yeah. Sarah."

"Who is she?"

Dylan looks back at the other boys who are trailing behind them and slows his pace down a little. She's just a friend who lived near me. She stuck by me the whole time I was in trouble. She knew everything that was going on. She was actually a witness when my case came up. Not that it mattered because I was locked up anyway. I never got a chance to thank her. Her father wouldn't let me talk to her. He moved away and made her change schools so I couldn't get near her. When Jay took me on the program I told him about it and he tried to help. He found out her new school and contacted her father but he told Jay he didn't want me near her.

"Well at least you tried mate."

"It's not that, with everything that's happened and all that stuff in the papers she might start believing it."

"Come on Dylan. If she knew what you went through and stuck by you all that time she's not going to change now."

"I know but I would just like the chance to talk to her. Even for a few minutes. You know, just to reassure her."

"Look Dylan the rest of these guys all think that this Ritchie is going to help them and everything will be fine so why don't we go along with it and see what happens. If nothing comes of it I'll go with you to the school and we'll find her for you."

Dylan stops walking and thinks for a few seconds.

"Okay, but don't tell any of the others about this."

"No problem mate." Adam says smiling.

The boys walk on until they reach the main road at the end of the industrial estate. Dylan's depressed mood appears to have lifted as he is now walking with a little spring in his step.

Across the road from them is the start of a small housing scheme and situated at the end of the row of houses is a large convenience store. Dylan looks around at the other boys. He nods at Adam and looks over at the store. Adam smiles back.

"Let's go." Adam says.

"Don't be stupid. The shop will be busy. We'll get caught." Stuart says. But Adam and Dylan are halfway across the busy road dodging the traffic. The rest of the boys follow and Stuart reluctantly runs to catch up with them.

As they approach the shop there are cars parked out in front with customers coming and going. Only Topher with his mischievous mind clocks that the engine of one of the cars is still running with no driver. Topher's old habits come back to him with a vengeance. With the thought of food on their minds and the excitement of raiding another shop the boys walk past the local newspaper advertising board without noticing the latest headline about them.

'£10,000 REWARD FOR INFORMATION LEADING TO THE ARREST OF NOTORIOUS GANG SUSPECTED OF MURDER'.

This was Williamson's latest brainwave. He had officially put up the ten thousand pounds reward on behalf of Jay and Jack's families for the safe capture of the boys. Unofficially, if the boys were found dead the reward would still be paid.

The boys enter the shop one at a time and separate up the aisles. At first they were almost unnoticed as the owner was busy serving a line of customers. The boys began filling their pockets with bars of chocolate and packets of biscuits. It wasn't until Casey went back up to the front of the shop to pick up a basket that one of the customers recognised him. He was standing in the queue looking over the front page of the evening newspaper while waiting to be served. He stared at the paper and then casually glanced around the shop catching a glimpse of some of the faces that were staring back at him from the paper. As Casey began filling the basket with ready made sandwiches from the open fridge the customer was informing the others in the queue of who the boys were. The police were informing the public not to approach the boys but the reward of ten thousand was too much to resist. This was Williamson's intention. Casey had filled the basket, the boys had filled their pockets and Dylan had filled his mouth. They were ready to go, ready to make their escape. Adam looked up at the checkout. The owner wasn't there. He looked over at the door. The owner had the keys in his hand ready to lock it. The other customers were standing near him ready for their share of the ten thousand. This was going to go bad, real bad, thought Adam. He looked over at the other boys and nodded at the door. The boys gathered at the top of the aisle out of sight of the front door.

"Guys there's six of us. We can take them."

Adams intentions were to charge at them and smash through the large window to escape.

"Where's Topher?"

The rest of the boys looked at each other and shrugged their shoulders. They start looking down the aisles when they hear a loud crash from the front of the shop. They look up to see the whole shop front caved in and the grille of a car sticking through it. The boys make a run for it. Adam smiles as he gets closer to the car and sees a pair of eyes struggling to see over the dashboard.

"TOPHER" Adam shouts.

He has the seat squeezed up tight to the steering wheel so that he can reach the pedals. He presses the clutch down and slams the gear stick into reverse.

"HURRY." he shouts.

The boys' faces light up as they scramble to get into the car.

The shop owner, along with the other customers, begins to give chase.

"THAT'S MY CAR." One of them shouts as he runs to catch them. After reversing out onto the road the shop owner stands in front of the car with his hands up to signal them to stop. Topher takes the gear stick out of reverse and puts it into first. He revs the engine and taunts the owner.

"What are you waiting for? Let's go." Casey shouts.

Topher looks at Adam who is in the front passenger seat.

"Don't worry. He'll move." Adam says.

Topher smiles and puts his foot on the accelerator until it touches the floor. The wheels screech as the car speeds off towards the shop owner. There is a split second stand off until the shop owner comes to his senses and realises that the car is not going to stop for him. His eyes widen and his jaw drops before he dives out of the way. Topher drives off and heads through the housing scheme until he reaches a main road. He cuts across this and continues until he finds a secluded area. They are hidden from any traffic but have a view of the streets at either side. Topher keeps the engine running to keep warm as the boys pass around the food and stuff their faces.

"Casey, close your mouth. You eat like a pig." Dylan says.

"No I don't."

"Yes you do." They all say together.

"Topher, how did you know to go for the car?" Adam asks.

"I clocked it sitting outside with the engine running and nobody was in it. Well when you guys entered the shop I noticed the newspaper board outside. It said ten thousand pounds reward for capture of the gang. When I entered I noticed the customers at the till watching you so I knew something was going to happen."

"I didn't even know you could drive. I would love to know how to steal a car." Naz says.

"How do you think he ended up in Borstal?" Dylan says.

"Really, is that right Topher?"

"Well not at first because it wasn't really stealing…more like taking a car without permission. That's what we used to do before we found out how to hot wire one. We would just kick a ball around outside the shops and every once in a while someone would come along that was in a hurry and think nothing of going into the shop and leaving the engine running. Then a friend of a friend showed us how to hotwire one and that's when the trouble started."

"Wait a minute guys. If that's true about the reward for our capture…then that means it's not just the police out looking for us. It's everyone." Stuart says.

"You're right. Anybody and everybody will be wanting their hands on that money." Casey says.

"So where do we go from here?" Topher asks.

"What about Ritchie. I thought we were going to see if he can help us." Naz replies.

"We've already been through this. They'll be watching him." says Adam.

"We can at least check it out. We have transport now."

"There's no harm in checking it out Adam." Dylan says. Adam shrugs. "Its up to you guys but I think it's a bad idea. Whatever we do, we have to get rid of this car or we'll be caught straight away."

"Aww but I've just got warmed up in here." Naz says.

"We can get another one. Did you not mention you wanted to know how to do it."

Adam looks at Topher who nods in agreement as he can't talk due to his mouthful of chocolate biscuits.

"Wait a minute. We've been walking about and hiding in sheds while all the time you could have been chauffeuring us around. Why didn't you mention this before?" Adam asks.

"Because Jay made me see the error of my ways" Dylan looks back at the other boys and laughs.

"You mean we are all on the run for murder...well triple murder, according to the papers and you are worried about being caught stealing a car."

The other boys all laugh except Topher.

"I can't figure you out Topher. I can't tell if you are really thick or if it's just an act to make people think you are thick." Adam says.

15.

As Smith drives up the road towards the convenience store he can see the commotion before he actually arrives. There are crowds of people gathered including reporters from nearly every newspaper in the country. He is starting to wonder if the people involved actually called the newspapers first and took their time to negotiate a fee for their story before they called the police. The barriers were set up around the shop and Smith was met by his partner who briefed him on the situation.

"Williamsons reward has only been in the paper for a few hours and already we have would-be heroes risking there lives for a few quid."

"I think it's a lot more than a few quid."

"What can we do? These boys are now going to be hunted like outlaws."

"Somehow I think that is Williamson's intention."

D.C. Nevin looks at him and nods in the direction over his shoulder. Not far from them is Smith's boss. Detective Chief Superintendent Watson, who is another one of Williamson's acquaintances. Nevin lowers her voice and they both
walk away.

"Have you heard about the conditions of the reward." She asks.

"Dead or alive?" Smith says as he shakes his head in disappointment.

"Wait until the papers get a hold of that one."

"Williamson will never admit to that."

As Smith looks around the scene he can't help but think about Billy. He knows he must have heard about what's going on here. He knows Billy and also knows he won't be able to resist coming back to help his brother. But Williamson's little stunt could be a problem. If anything happens to those boys he's blown any chance of catching him. If Billy is anything like what he used to be, he will want revenge.

"We've set up road blocks at every exit out of the city in case they've swapped cars…well, now that we know they can drive." Nevin informs Smith.

"That's wasting our resources."

"What do you mean Inspector?"

"Those boys aren't going anywhere. If they can drive they would have been gone long ago. You have to try and think like these boys. They're not stupid; they've grown up being chased by the police. That car will have been dumped by now so our best chance is to search the schemes and back streets. We can maybe work out where the boys are heading if we find the car. They'll be on foot and my guess is either Frank's or Bruce's. If they knew it was Williamson who was behind all this I would head straight there and wait for them to show up.

Keep surveillance at their addresses and let me know about anything unusual".

***

The boys sit in silence as they watch a patrol car drive past them then do a u turn in the main the road before driving past them again.

"I think we should swap cars now." Adam says.

"Yeah I think that would be a good idea." Topher adds.

The boys step out of the warm car into the cold night and cross the road into a quiet street. Topher leads the way as the boys follow him into someone's garden. On the way around the back Topher picks up a brick and walks straight over to the garden shed and smashes the padlock, one that is designed to keep people like Topher from getting inside.

"Topher what the hell are you doing?" Stuart says.

"Thought you guys needed a car?"

"We do."

"Well, we need some tools."

Stuart doesn't answer and leaves Topher to it as he searches around in the darkness and comes across a tool box. He pulls it out of the shed so that he can see better in the moonlight. He picks up a screwdriver and carefully tries to put the toolbox back into the same place he found it. He closes the door and walks away with the rest of the boys following him. Before he reaches the front garden he picks up a large stone. With Topher still out in front, they walk through to a busier street up ahead.

"Topher, there's loads of cars in that quiet street why don't you get one of those?" Casey asks.

"Think about what you've just said."

"What do you mean?"

"Quiet street. Window smashing. Does that not register?"

The boys come across a small dark path with over grown bushes.

"Right we'll wait here. Topher, go get us a car. Dylan you go with him and keep a look out for any nosey neighbours." Adam says.

The two boys walk up the street while the others watch them through the gaps in the bushes. Dylan walks up to the first car and looks over at Topher.

"No not that one. Come on across the road." Topher whispers.

Dylan follows him and stops at a newer car that has extra large wheels and a few dents in the front and sides. Topher shakes his head. Dylan looks at him puzzled.

"Will you just hurry up and pick a car." He says angrily.

Topher looks up the street. Two cars away from where they are standing he sees what he is looking for.

"That one, that's the one we want."

"Topher can you please tell me what was wrong with those ones?" Dylan says looking back at the row of cars.

"Well the first one was a wreck which means the owner doesn't have much cash to buy a new one, therefore he probably doesn't have much cash to buy fuel. Meaning we won't get very far in it. The sporty one you pointed out with the big wheels and the stupid looking bumpers has a few dents in it which means the owner has ripped the arse out of it. For one thing it attracts too much attention which we definitely do not need and another possibility, we might not get very far. Now this one." he says as he shatters the small window in the back using the brick.

"This one is not much to look at considering it is a fairly new one. It has a boring shape and is polished to a high standard. It doesn't have the fancy wheels or body kit that draws attention to it. Some people might say it's an old fuddy duddy's car."

Topher continues as he feels along the windows unlocking each door. He slides into the driver's seat and smashes the steering column using the brick and screwdriver. He then jams the screwdriver into the ignition and turns it as if he's turning a key. The engine starts. He reaches over to the other side and unlocks the passenger door for Dylan.

"Now if you think about it, this car is well maintained and if you care to look at this little dial here it will signal a full tank of petrol. Which I suspect the owner keeps for emergencies. Emergencies like ours."

"Little smart ass" Dylan mumbles as he signals for the others to come over.

The rest of the boys run towards the car and the four boys squeeze into the back.

Topher is busy flicking through the owners cassette tapes.

"Topher what are you doing? Let's go." Dylan shouts.

"Just a minute. I've got have the correct music for driving."

Dylan turns around and looks at the others in the back. He puts his hands up with his palms facing up to signal his confusion. Stuart shrugs his shoulders and does the same back.

"Ah here we are. The Rolling Stones. I knew the owner had to have something good in his life."

He slams the tape into the stereo.

"A good Stones tape will see you through bad times more than a flashy car ever will." He says before turning up the volume and driving off.

"You're really weird Topher. You know that?" Casey says.

Topher ignores the comment and continues trying to see over the steering wheel.

"So where are we going then guys?" Topher asks.

"I think we should go to Rich's." Stuart says.

"No way. You know he'll be getting watched. They'll be sitting waiting on us." Adam says.

"Look guys. I need to know which way to go."

"Just drive Topher. We'll work it out as we go." Dylan says.

Topher takes a few turns and finds a main road.

"Follow the city centre signs; at least if we do decide to go to Rich's I know the way from there."

"I say we just hit the road and drive until we're in another city and no-one knows us." Topher says.

"Yeah cause our faces are only in every newspaper in the country." Naz says quite cheekily.

"Well we'll just go to another country."

"That sounds good to me, as long as I get to drive."

Upon reaching the city centre all the boys are arguing about where to go. Except Topher, who chooses a lane in the road and follows it round. The rest of the boys don't realise until it's too late. He turns up onto the Tay road bridge.

"Topher, where are you going?" Dylan shouts.
Topher smiles and puts the foot down. As the car turns on the bend he speeds up even more.

"I think you guys had better duck down." Topher says as he turns up the stereo and puts the accelerator pedal to the floor.

"Topher stop. No." Stuart shouts

The car races towards the checkpoint and in a split second the boys all look at the barrier as it approaches and then scramble to lower their heads. The car smashes through the barrier and cracks the windscreen. The boys all lift their heads and look out as Topher eases his foot off the pedal to slow down slightly as they cross the bridge.

"I always wanted to do that." He says after he turns down the stereo.

"What? Did you need loud music to accompany it?" Adam says as all the boys laugh.

"Well the way I see it is. In years to come whenever you hear that song you're always going to remember this moment."

"I can't believe you just did that." Stuart says.

"At least you've stopped arguing about where we're going. And I never heard you complaining when I crashed through the shop window."

"So where are we going?"

"Yeah Topher. Where are we going?" Naz asks.

"I don't know I just thought that maybe we should get out of the city for a while so we don't have to keep watching our backs every second."

"And crashing through a barrier on the Tay Bridge is really the way to go about it." Stuart says sarcastically.

"Do you actually know which direction to go when we get across here?" Dylan asks.

"No. I've never been across here. Have any of the rest of you guys?"

They all in turn reply no and Topher just smiles. He reaches the end of the bridge and goes around the roundabout twice before making a decision to turn off at the next left. He follows the road round until he comes to a junction. The sign has an arrow pointing to the left for Newport and another pointing right for Tayport.

"Okay Topher. Which one are we following?" Adam asks.

Topher is busy looking around and taking in the surroundings but eventually looks up at the sign.

"Oh. Eh. Newport." He says as he turns left.

"Why? What's in Newport?"

"You'll see."

"I thought you said you hadn't been here before."

"I haven't."

"We'll how do you know what's there."

"I don't. I'm just following the lights."

"What lights?"

Topher doesn't answer but drives at a snail's pace along the narrow road. Adam looks around and realises what Topher is doing.

"Are those the lights you're following?"

"What lights? What are you guys talking about?" Stuart says.

"Take a look to your right guys." Adam says.

"Wow look at that." Dylan says.

All the boys' heads turn and look over the river. Topher pulls up and parks the car at the side of the road and the boys stare in amazement at the view of Dundee from Fife.

"What? Have you guys never seen that before?" Casey says.

"No, never" Dylan answers.

Topher drives on further along the road and turns up to the left. He parks the car in a dead end with the smashed front facing a wall. The boys get out and walk back to the main road. Dylan points to a gap in the wall which takes them to a large grass area. They walk to the steep edge near the river and look down as the waves crash against the rocks. Topher sits down on the grass with his feet dangling over the edge and stares out at the city all lit up in the night sky.

"I'll bet you can sit there for hours looking at that." Adam says as he sits down next to him.

"I can. It looks a lot different from up there." Dylan says pointing up to the Law hill before he finds a space to sit at the other side of Topher.

"I've sat up there many times and often wondered what it would look like from over here."

The rest of the boys also sit down and not a word is said as they watch the commotion at the start of the bridge. Police cars, with their lights flashing and sirens blaring, race across the bridge as if they are in hot pursuit of the boys and minutes later race back again. The boys are used to the noise now and become oblivious to it as they sit for a long time in silence enjoying the view which is accompanied with the fresh sea air. They each drift away with their own deep thoughts and block out the harsh reality of their situation.

"So, really guys. What's our next move?" Naz asks.

"We need to go get a different car?" Topher says.

"No. I mean where are we going from here?"

"Are you deaf as well as stupid? He says we're going to get another car." Casey says.

"Stupid? That's good coming from you."

Both boys stand up and have their faces only inches away from each other.

"Get out of my face Paki." Casey says as he pushes Naz away.

Naz takes a quick step and charges forward with his head down. Both boys land on the ground, wrestling and punching each other. Dylan sighs and looks over at Stuart.

"Back to reality huh."

They get up and separate them.

Once the boys calm down they all sit facing each other as they discuss their options.

"Well I would be up for getting another car and driving as far away from here as we can." Topher says.

"And do what?" Adam asks.

"I don't know I've never been anywhere else."

"Me neither." Dylan says.

"What about you Casey?"

"I went a lot of places with my mum but I was too young to remember much about it or even where we went. My dad was always too busy working to even take me to the park never mind out of Dundee."

"Naz?"

"I've obviously been to India a few times with my family but I haven't travelled to another town."

The rest of the boys look at Stuart.

"What? What's this all about Adam?"

"Well, I'm just making a point that none of us have ever really left Dundee before. We don't know our way around any other city. We won't know anyone which means we can't trust anyone. Each of us has grown up here in different areas of the city. We know the streets and the places to hide." Adam's little speech had an ulterior motive. He wants to keep the boys together and to persuade them to go after Frank and Bruce.

"So what do we do here Adam? I mean we can't run and hide forever."

"Well we haven't done anything wrong. We have to find a way to prove that. I think we should go after Frank and Bruce."

"And do what?"

Adam would love to say kill them like they killed Jay but he plays it cool.

"We capture one of them and force him to tell the truth about killing Jay."

"Yeah, that sounds good to me. To hell with this running and hiding caper. Let's go after them." Casey says.

"A small problem though. We don't know where they live." Dylan says.

"I know someone who could probably help us out there." Stuart says.

The boys all look at Adam who smiles back.

"So that's our plan. We go to Rich's. He can help us get Franks and Bruce's addresses and we capture one and make him tell the police what really happened." Dylan says quite confident that everything will go to plan.
The boys look back out over the water and can see the disruption they have caused is still going on.

"I think we should stay here a little bit longer guys." Casey says.

"Yeah I think maybe that would be a good idea." Stuart says.

The boys sit for a while longer before Topher disappears and comes back with another car. The rest of the boys pile in as he casually drives back over the bridge unnoticed by the uniformed police who are still on guard keeping the reporters from the scene.

"Right, take a left when we get off this road Topher." Dylan says as he directs the way to Rich's flat.

After a few wrong turns Dylan eventually finds his way to the correct street.

"You sure you know where you're going Dylan." Adam asks.

"Yeah, this is it here. I only ever went to Rich's twice with Jay when we were heading out from the city centre."

Topher drives up and down the street slowly looking for any policemen that may be watching his place. They notice an unmarked car with two men watching the front door to Rich's block. Topher drives far down the street and parks behind a large works van. From one end of the street the car is totally hidden from view.

"Right, Dylan. You go and see if he's in." Adam says.
"Stuart you come with me."
"Why?"

"What do you mean why? Because this was you're idea. He's your mate and you argued hard enough for us to come here." Dylan demands.

The boys all look at each other in shock as Stuart mumbles to himself after being put in his place.

The two boys creep around the block of flats and enter through the back door.

"Which floor is it?"

"I don't know. I never came in here. Jay always went in on his own, I always waited in the van."

"Great."

Stuart checks the names on the doors as they both run up the flights of stairs. They stop on the third floor.

"Bryson. Here it is." Stuart says catching his breath.
He flicks the letter box and in a few seconds Rich opens the door and stares at him.

"What are you guys doing here? Do you know how much trouble you're in?"

"Rich. We're stuck mate. We really need you're help." Stuart pleads.

"I can't help you. You're wanted for triple murder."

"Come on Rich. You know we didn't do that."

"How am I supposed to help you?"

"Look, can we come in and talk. There are policemen watching from outside."

Rich hesitates for a few seconds and opens the door wider to let them pass. Stuart walks in but Dylan turns to go back down the stairs.

"Where are you going?"

"I'll have to go tell the others."

"What they're all here? They can't all come up here."

Dylan ignores him and keeps on going. Rich tries to shout after him again but he doesn't answer.

"What the hell happened Stuart?" Rich asks.
Stuart is about to answer but he looks around the room and clocks the large T.V. and stereo.

"You must have a really good job mate." he says changing the subject.

"Yeah, I have a good job. Now what happened at the camp?"

"What is your job?"

"I do odd jobs for the council."

"What kind of jobs?"

"Never mind my job Stuart."

Stuart looks right at Rich

"They killed Jay Rich."

"Who?"

"You know who, Frank and Bruce."

"Did you see them do it?"

"No, Adam did."

"Who's Adam?"

"The new guy who replaced you on the program"

"Who killed the other two?"

"Dylan's uncle was an accident. We don't know who killed Jack."

"But you were seen running from his house."

"He was dead when we got there, I swear."

"We went there to get him to help us but he was lying face down on his bed. It looked like he had been strangled. His whole house had been trashed."

The rest of the boys walk into the flat and waste no time in making themselves at home. Rich is immediately irritated by his unwelcome guests who have taken over his flat.

"You guys can't stay here. I'm being watched."

"Yeah, we know. We saw them out front. They were too

Youngsters

busy chatting and drinking their coffee to notice anything." Casey says.

"Look guys, how do you actually expect me to help you? Do you know there's a reward for your capture? It's ten thousand pounds."

"Yeah, we thought we would be worth more than that. But then again we do have a Paki with us which kind of does bring the price down a bit." Casey says.

Naz is about to go for Casey but Rich steps in.

"No, you're not starting this in here. I'm warning you. I can't believe you two are still at it."

"Still at it? They're worse than ever." Stuart says.

"Do you know that unofficially the reward is going to be paid out if you are captured dead or alive?" Rich says as the room goes silent.
The boys look at each other in shock.

"The reward was only issued this morning and already there's talk of people coming to Dundee from different parts of the country to try and track you down. I think you guys should go and hand yourselves in now before one, or even all of you, are killed."

Stuart looks around the room at the rest of the boys' faces to see their reaction but they all look at Adam. He shrugs his shoulders and looks back at Stuart then nods in the direction of Rich.

"What's going on?" Rich says.

"Rich we need a favour." Stuart says.

"What kind of favour?"

Stuart pauses and looks around at the other boys.

"We need you to get Frank's and Bruce's addresses."

"What? You can't be serious."

"They killed Jay. We think they killed Jack as well but…"

"So what are you guys going to do? Go and kill them."

"That's not a bad idea." Adam says.

The rest of the boys smile at Adam but he keeps a straight face.

"Rich we're being blamed for Jay's murder and they did it so we need to get them to confess." Stuart says.

"So what are you going to do knock on their door and ask them to tell the truth?"

"Well, not exactly, more like force them."

Rich stands shaking his head at them.

"And what do you think Jay would say to all this?"

The boys look at each other and then look to the floor.

"Do you guys know it's his funeral tomorrow?"

"Are you going?"

"Do you think we could go?" Dylan asks looking at Adam.

The other boys also look at Adam and Rich picks up on this. He looks over at Stuart with staring eyes wondering what is going on.

"It will be swarming with police and reporters. They would pick us out in seconds." Adam says as he gives Dylan a wink on the sly so that none of the other boys see him. Dylan smiles to himself.

Rich was under the impression that Stuart would take over as leader when he left but now realises that Adam is now the leader and not Stuart. He also realises that they are never going to hand themselves in as things have gone too far now. Williamson's face flashes in his mind and he doesn't want to imagine what he would do to him if he is caught helping them.

"He's right. They'll be expecting you guys to turn up at the funeral. Why don't you stay here when I go and I'll try and get the addresses for you?" Rich says unconvincingly.

"So you'll help us." Stuart says.

"I can't promise anything, but I'll see what I can do."

16.

Mr Tony Walker had run a successful building firm in the city for many years. He had taken over the firm from his father and built it up in the hope of passing it on to his own son, Casey. In the early eighties when his father was still running the firm the work began to dry up and the business started to suffer. He would work late with his father every night and most weekends. They knew the work would pick up eventually but in the meantime the only contact he had with his son was at breakfast. He would arrive home long after Casey had gone to bed and through his absence his marriage was also beginning to suffer. As the work picked up, due to his father securing large expensive contracts with the local council, it was too late. His wife was already in the middle of a full blown affair. She broke the news that she was leaving him for another man, an Asian man.

Casey had taken the news very badly as his mother had walked away without an explanation or even saying goodbye. This eventually took its toll on Tony and Casey and their 'father and son' relationship began to drift apart. They argued constantly and this drove Tony to work late again to avoid contact with him. Casey was always being sent home from school which made his father angry due to him having to be called away from work. Tony spoiled Casey. Anything he asked for he would get. Each time he was in trouble and they argued he would feel guilty and then buy him expensive gifts to make up for it. He did it in business every day.

Workers not happy, give them a pay rise. Problem solved. Customers not happy, reduce their bill. Problem solved. His kid playing up, give him some cash. Problem not solved.

Tony got to know Jason Fallon many years ago after he came to him with a request to help with fundraising, for whatever event he was trying to organise at the time and they both struck up a friendship. Tony, like most people who knew Jay, had a lot of respect for the work he did in helping youngsters who had lost their way. Tony had heard about The Program and the constant rejections from the council Board. He knew Williamson would be behind it. He had enough dealings with him over the years to know what he said in those meetings. And the other Board members, through fear, agreed with everything he said.

With the constant threat of his son being taken away and put into a boys' home he saw an opportunity to maybe help him and Jay. He put forward his proposal of funding the program himself. With the condition that if the program proved to be successful over a period of two years he would fund it for a further three. Tony made this information public which put the Board under enormous pressure as to having a reasonable explanation as to why it would be rejected. Williamson didn't care he still rejected it without any explanation. But the other Board members approved it. They were scared of Williamson but they had no option but to vote against him.

In the first six months of the program Tony had heard good reports from Jay about his son's progress but the racial hatred was still a problem. Tony had sat his son down many times and tried to talk to him but when a boy's mother leaves him to run off with an Asian man there was not really much advice that he could give him. He hoped that he would eventually accept it but it would take time.

In the last month, before the boys found themselves on the run, Tony had received two phone calls from Casey. For the first time in a long time he was able to talk to him without arguing. On his second phone call Casey had actually told him that he missed him. After Tony hung up the phone he broke down.

Since the boys had been on the run, Tony had overheard the comments about his son. Whether he was at work or down at his local pub he knew people were pointing the finger and blaming him. Saying it was all his fault for the way Casey had turned out. He ignored most of them, simply because he knew they were right. But there was one thing he knew his son wasn't, and that was a murderer. He knew Casey respected Jay as did all the other boys he had tried to help. And for them to turn on him, well something just didn't add up.

On his way home from work he stopped off at his local newsagents for cigarettes. He also picked up a copy of the evening paper. He knew it would be filled with the usual comments from the public saying that society has no time for these boys. They were given a chance and blew it. They should be locked up for good and made an example of. He hated these people who judged his son and the rest of the boys because they believed the overblown press stories. They were basically making them out to be guilty before any of the boys had a chance to say exactly what really happened. He arrived home and threw the paper on the dinning table and went to the kitchen to prepare his dinner. On his return he slid his plate down and pulled the paper over. He took a small bite of his steak pie as he scanned the headline. He nearly choked as he stared at the caption about the reward for the gang. The story was accompanied with a photo of Councillor Williamson. He pushed his plate aside as he read on, in anger. When he moved to the bottom of the page, in bold letters, was 'Continued on page 13.' He quickly flicked through and opened it up. Inside there were more photos of the boys and another of Williamson holding a cheque which was blown up in the next photo so that the reader could see the amount clearly. His phone started ringing. Still clutching the paper he marched over to answer it. It was his younger brother Graham.

"I tried the office they said you had left. I guess you heard the news."

"What? About the reward? Yeah, I heard but I don't know what the hell Williamson's playing at."

"I guess you don't know then."

"Know what?"

"The reward, unofficially, is apparently going to be paid out…Dead or alive."

The line goes silent. Tony felt like he was about to be sick.

"Tony. You still there?"

"Yeah, I'm still here." He answers in a croaky voice as if he is about to break down.

"Can he do that?"

"Tony, he's already been on the early news denying it, saying it's just people stirring things up. He says he has released the reward for the boys own safety so that they are caught as soon as possible."

"He's obviously going to deny it."

"Obviously"

"Putting up that reward is basically saying that they are all guilty. I'm sick of it."

"This is about to turn into a bloody manhunt."

"I'm going to go and see Williamson in the morning."

"Do you know its Jason Fallon's funeral tomorrow?"

"Oh great. Williamson has timed that perfectly hasn't he? The press will have this built up and everyone will be talking about catching them. I'll make sure I turn up early tomorrow because I know he'll be at work before it."

"Do you want me to come with you?"

"No, it's okay. I've dealt with him a few times before."

"Okay but give me a call when you get up if you change your mind."

Tony hangs up the phone and looks over at his dinner. He takes the plate and scrapes the food into the bin. He'll maybe eat something later if he gets his appetite back. He goes into the living room and flicks the channels on the T.V. The news is not scheduled for hours yet so he tries to relax. He phones the hotline number he was given from the police when they came to visit. He asks for Smith. After ranting and raving for a few minutes Smith manages to calm him down. He explains to him that he agrees with everything he has said and sympathises with him but there is nothing he can do as Williamson is not breaking any laws. Smith is very blunt and to the point as he has had non-stop calls since the evening paper was published.

"So what's this about the reward being paid out if the boys are found dead or alive?"

"Where did you receive that information?"

"It doesn't matter where. I want to know what you are doing about it?"

"Mr Walker. I can assure you that if we had evidence that someone was going to pay an individual to take the law into their own hands we would arrest them. We have received the same information as yourself and we are working on it. We need to trace the source of this information. We will also be questioning Councillor Williamson as to his knowledge of this information."

"So by the time you get around to questioning him any idiot with access to a gun can shoot and kill my son knowing they will be £10,000 better off." Tony said before slamming the phone down.

It rang back within seconds but Tony ignored it. He went to the fridge and opened a bottle of beer. Twenty minutes later he opened another as he sat staring at the television. The whole night he sat in deep thought about his son as he drank beer after beer until he passed out on the couch. He woke early in the morning in an uncomfortable position with the T.V. still on. He lay for a while as he flicked the remote through each channel hoping for some good news about his son. He unsteadily made his way to the kitchen and put the kettle on. He had to pull himself together. He was about to pay Williamson a visit. After some strong coffee he had a shower and quickly drove to the council offices. He knew he was early and Williamson wouldn't even be there yet but if he didn't do it this way he would never get in to see him. Williamson could give people the run around for days, even weeks if need be. He parked his car and made his way to the large entrance. The security and receptionists had been well briefed. They were practically in his face as he walked through the door. They took his name and gave him an appointment time for later that day, an appointment that would never be kept. There would be a list of excuses as to why Williamson wouldn't be there. He waited outside. Ten minutes had past and it started to get busy. A large group of office workers who were chatting away walked in, and Tony walked with them. The security looked up slightly and noticing they were workers he put his head back down to continue reading his newspaper. Tony walked straight past and as the group of women gathered to wait at the lift he made a sharp exit to the stairs. When he reached the top level he peered through a gap in the door. There was another security guard outside Williamson's door. Tony walked around chatting to numerous women, all of whom were glad to have some attention before they proceeded with there monotonous typing and paperwork. His plan was to sneak into Williamson's office and wait on him arriving but as he looked through the gap again his face dropped. Williamson was already in. He walked from his office to one of the women and handed her some folders. He had forgotten how intimidating Williamson's appearance was. He questioned his actions for a split second then thought about his son. He marched through the door.

"Williamson I want to talk to you." He said in a raised voice, the place went quiet and everyone looked up. The security guard stormed over and put his hands out to grab him.

"Take your hands away from me right now." Tony demanded.

The security guard looked at Williamson who waved him away. With the amount of press hanging about due to Jay's funeral the last thing he needed was a scene. He knew if Tony had been thrown out of the building with the reporters hanging around outside he would gladly stand and give them a statement criticising him. The security guard backed off and Tony continued walking towards Williamson.

"Come on, we'll talk in my office." He said with his large sneering grin.

He told a young girl outside his door to hold all his calls as he walked past. As soon as the door closed behind them Tony's rage was ready to explode.

"What the hell are you playing at?" Tony shouted and

turned to look at him with fire in his eyes.

He had prepared himself for a heated argument. He had prepared himself for Williamson.

"Calm down Tony. Take a seat and I'll explain." Williamson walked behind his desk and sat in his large leather chair. It was positioned to keep him upright but his weight still made him sink back allowing his gut to hang out. Tony was still standing and Williamson gestured for him to sit. Tony reluctantly sat down. The chair was so comfortable he reluctantly felt at ease as he sat back. This was not going to plan.

"So what's this all about?"

"What do you mean? You practically put a bounty on my son's head."

"Hardly, I put up a reward for the boys' own good. We can't have teenage boys running around the city killing innocent people."

"Dead or alive, you're going to pay up."

Williamson laughed and shook his head.

"Do you honestly believe that if someone killed those boys that I'm going to pay them £10,000? Seriously?"

"Oh I know you won't pay it. But I know you released the information so that other people will believe it."

"Tony, Tony." He says shaking his head.

"You of all people should know that you don't believe everything you hear."

Tony stood up.

"I'll tell you what. If anything happens to my son I'm going to come after you Blair. All those dodgy dealings that you think are covered up will soon surface."

Williamson stayed calm.

"Is that right? Well…let me see, what about you're building firm..?"

"What about it?"

"Where do you think you got all those contracts and cheap supplies? Actually where do you think you're old man got the contracts to start up the business in the first place?"

"My father built that business through hard work." Williamson laughs and stands up.

"I think it's time for you to leave and go pay your father a visit."

Tony's throat was dry. He wanted to lash out at Williamson. Although he didn't fear him as much as most people he knew he was no match for him. He turned around and walked out of the office and past the women who were trying hard not to look at him. His face was like thunder. He knew where he was heading and it was not to his work. He wanted to know the truth.

He knocked on the door of his parent's house and his mother answered.

"Tony, what's wrong? Is it Casey?"

"No, no, he's still on the run. Well, as far as I know."

"I just need a word with dad."

"He's watching T.V. would you like some breakfast?"

"Yeah, that would be good, thanks."

Tony wasn't hungry but he wanted his mother out of the way while he talked to his father.

"Hey dad"

"Tony. What's happened is it Casey?"

"No. It's not Casey. I need a word with you dad."

Tony's father put the volume down on the T.V. and turned to face him."

"I need a straight answer dad. It's about the business. My son's life could be at stake here."

"Sure, what is it?"

"The contracts" "The early ones when you started out. Were they legitimate?"

"What do you mean?"

"Don't muck me around dad; you know exactly what I'm asking. I've just left Williamson's office."

He looked at his father straight in the eyes and he could tell what was coming. His father shook his head. He tried to explain but Tony stood up.

"You had better go see a solicitor because it's all away to come out."

"But How? Why?"

"Because he's not about to get away with putting a price on my son's head."

Tony goes to leave.

"Where are you going?"

"To dig up the contracts that were made since I took over the business, because I'm certainly not going down for it."

17.

Billy stepped off the large cargo ship when it arrived at Liverpool docks. He had arranged it with a friend and paid cash. No questions asked. Security was minimal and the authorities were more concerned with inspecting the shipment than the crew on board. Billy hated sailing and had thrown up several times during the journey. He found this very ironic considering he worked with boats. The same ship would have two more long journeys before it would arrive back in the same dock. It had been discussed between Billy and the crew of the possibility of an extra person joining him on the return journey. With the mention of more money, a nod of the head accompanied with a large smile was enough to convince Billy the deal was done. He left the docks and walked to the nearest taxi rank. He instructed the driver to take him to the train station. He checked the train times, the next one to Edinburgh was not leaving for another hour yet. He phoned Kevin to let him know of his expected arrival time in Edinburgh and to ask him to make arrangements for him to be picked up and driven the rest of the way to Dundee. He would have travelled on the train direct to Dundee but Kevin had the station checked out. Smith has several police officers manning the exit. The photos of him in the paper were over ten years old. They were from the last time he was in police custody and although he looked different there's a possibility that a sharp eyed officer could pick him out. They decided not to take the risk. Billy went to the newsagents and picked up two papers, paid for them and then walked through to the bar. He ordered himself a pint of Tennents, something he hadn't tasted in a long time. Some of the islands bars imported it in during the holiday season but he had become accustomed to the San Miguel years before. He sat by the bar with his cap pulled down over his forehead. He thought about finding a secluded corner but felt this would attract more attention to him. He took a drink from his pint and picked up one of the newspapers. The front page had run a large photo of a smashed shop front with the headline relating to the boys or gang as they are now known. He quickly reads the story before turning a few pages where there is a double page spread of the shop owner telling his exaggerated story of how he risked his life to capture the violent gang. There is another photo of the getaway car which was found hours later and only two miles from the shop. The photo showed the car doors left open with the keys still in the ignition. There are biscuit wrappers and empty crisp packets strewn over the seats and floor. Billy smiles as he thinks about the police rushing around organising a major search operation while the boys are parked up somewhere having a picnic in the car. His smile disappears as he turns to the next page to read a statement from Smith telling people not to risk their lives for the reward that's being offered by Councillor Williamson. Billy then starts to think about the would-be heroes out to catch them. He knows he has to find Adam soon. He looks at his watch and finishes his pint before walking off towards the platform.

***

The boys find they can relax for one night. They clean themselves up and have some proper food followed by a good nights sleep. By morning they are up early and gathered around Rich's newly acquired large T.V. to watch the latest news about themselves. The video footage of the stolen car smashing through the barrier is shown in slow motion.

"Look you can just about see Topher's head." Naz says.

"Hey Topher, were you actually ducking or is that you sitting upright?" Casey says.

The boys all laugh and even Rich, who is getting himself prepared for facing Williamson manages to give a smile. He walks out of his flat smartly dressed in a new suit that was purchased only days before and dodged around more questions about his new job. He had hardly slept as he tossed and turned at the dilemma of betraying his friends or crossing Williamson. His chest is tight and his stomach is in knots and feels as though he is about to throw up. He leans over a wall and retches but nothing comes up. On the way to the taxi rank he smokes another cigarette. His third since he got out of bed. He'd stopped when he was on the program but had started again due to the stress of recent events. The temptation to go back to harder substances was there at the back of his mind but at the moment he had the will power to resist. He was on his way to pay his respects to someone who would be so ashamed of him right now. Jay had done so much for him but he had let the influence of Williamson and a bundle of money take over…a large bundle of money.

"Right guys let's go." Adam says as he looks out of the window to see Rich walking away in the distance and the unmarked car following not far behind.

"Where are we going? I thought we were staying here until Rich comes back." Naz asks.

"We are going to pay our respects."

"We can't go there, you said yourself the place will be swarming with police."

"Don't worry about it, we'll keep our distance."

Adam looks at Topher and nods.

"You ready?"

Topher takes the car keys out of his pocket and jingles them.

Rich is dropped off on the main road as the traffic is so busy due to the amount of people attending the funeral. He is starting to feel the effects of the cigarettes and the amount of nicotine in his system is making him nauseas. He recognises a few people up ahead of him and walks fast to catch up with them. As he almost reaches them he slows down and trails on behind as they reach the gardens and join the large crowd that has gathered. He notices Frank and Bruce standing together in their security uniforms. He puts his head down and moves in tight to the crowd hoping they won't see him. The hearse appears at the entrance and the small group of reporters begin clicking away their cameras. There is a procession of cars trailing behind and one of them is the Lord Provost's limousine. As Jay's family walk behind the coffin the driver of the limo steps out and opens the rear door. The Lord Provost steps out and the clicking of cameras begins again. The opposite door opens and Rich's face freezes and his eyes widen with fear as Williamson's head appears above the car.

The large crowd of people soon disappears through the large wooden doors of the crematorium and this gives the police and reporters time to relax. At the other side of the building, through the trees and bushes, the boys sit watching and waiting. The doors close after the last of the people go in and the police make their way to the exit on the other side of the building. Nearly forty five minutes pass before the exit doors open.

"Right guys you go back to the car and wait on me and I'll see which car we have to follow." Adam says.

"I'll stay with you." Dylan says.

"Oh and Topher, keep the engine running we may have to move fast."

Adam and Dylan peer through the bushes as they watch each and every person coming out.

"Look there's Rich." Dylan says.

The two boys watch him talking with someone and the crowd breaks up a little. Rich goes to walk away and Frank comes into view. They talk for a few minutes as Rich looks around nervously. Frank gestures to someone else and then a large beast of a man comes over. Rich now looks scared and appears to be pleading with them, then the large man puts his arm around Rich and pats him on the back. Bruce joins them and they smile at each other before the large man walks off.

"What's going on Adam?"

"Shhh, I don't know."

Frank writes something on a card and hands it to Rich. Somehow I don't think it will be safe for us to go back to Rich's place do you?" Dylan comments.

Adam doesn't answer but watches closely as Rich walks off while Frank and Bruce head towards the car park.

"Get ready Dylan we'll have to move real fast."
Frank and Bruce both get into the same car and Frank is driving.

"Right let's go." Adam says as he scrambles back under the bushes and through the gap in the wire fence that they had made earlier. They can see Topher sitting at the wheel with the engine running, ready to go. Adam goes in the front this time and Casey sits on the floor to let Dylan squeeze into the back. Topher drives around onto the main road and parks up near the exit to the car park. They sit in silence as they watch Frank's car pull out and drive along the main road away from them. Topher goes to follow.

"No, wait. Keep your distance. If he looks in his mirror he'll see us straight away." Adam says.

Topher lets a few cars go past then pulls out. There is a long queue of traffic that is moving very slowly and the boys start to panic when they see a policeman up ahead. He is holding back the crowds and traffic to allow some of the cars to exit the car park. As they approach the policeman they look straight ahead and Topher prepares himself to do a u turn across the middle of the road if necessary. The policeman waves them past and the boys all laugh as he is too busy concentrating on what's going on around him to notice who was actually driving.

With the boys not far behind, Frank drives into the Dryburgh area of the city and stops. Topher pulls in quickly behind a parked car and they all watch as Bruce gets out.

"Hey I know where we are, I used to live not far from here." Stuart says.

Frank drives on and Topher moves slowly past. They watch Bruce enter his house and then Topher speeds up to catch up with Frank. He drives onto the dual carriageway and Topher struggles to keep up as he rips along the road. They come to a roundabout and an argument starts about which direction he went as they loose sight of his car.

"Over there. Quick." Naz shouts pointing to a road on the right.

In the distance they can see the tail of his car going up a small hill and turning left. Topher puts the foot down and the wheels screech as he turns the car sharp around the corner.

"You guys duck. There he is." Adam shouts, as he turns his back to the window to hide his and Topher's faces. Frank is outside of his car locking the door and doesn't take much notice as the boys speed past him.

"Do you think he saw us?" Naz asks.

"I don't think so." Adam says as he looks back to see Frank walking casually towards his house.

"Somehow, I think if he saw us he'd be back in his car following us." Casey answers.

"So what's next? Where do we go from here?" Topher asks.

Adam smiles. "We go back and wait on Rich."

"Are you sure Adam? I mean after what we saw earlier. Do you really think that would be a good idea?" Dylan says.

Why? What did you see?" Casey asks.

Dylan goes to speak but Adam turns and looks at him and shakes his head.

"Uh eh, it was nothing. It doesn't matter." Dylan mumbles.

The boys turn up back at Rich's and the unmarked police car has not returned yet. They find a space to park out of view but also where they can see Rich's block of flats. They watch as he strolls down the road looking like he has the weight of the world on his shoulders. Casey goes to get out of the car.

"Where are you going? Get back in." Adam demands.

"Why? He's home. Let's go."

"We're not going in. He'll be back out in a few minutes watch."

Dylan nods at Casey to confirm that Adam is right.

"Can I at least get out and stretch my legs. It's alright for you. You've got the front seat; you're not the one stuck on the floor in the back of the car."

"Okay but be quick."

"Yes sir." Casey says quite cheekily.

Just as Adam had said, Rich appears back out of his block and is walking fast up his street.

"Casey get in quick. Topher start the car." Adam shouts. Rich is walking at a fast pace away from his flat. He has to get to a phone box and explain to Frank that the boys have gone.

"Hey, Rich. Where are you off to in such a hurry?" Adam says as Topher drives up beside him.

"Oh eh just off to see a mate."

"Squeeze in we'll give you a lift."

"I won't fit in there. There's not enough room in the back."

"That's okay the back folds down and Casey can climb into the boot from there?"

"Nah, Naz is smaller than me, he can do it. He's used to travelling that way anyway" Casey says as he has a laugh to himself.

Naz doesn't find it funny and lunges forward throwing a punch. Dylan tries to intervene and the punch clips the top of Casey's head. Casey jumps out of the car and starts taunting Naz to a fight.

"Right Casey get in the boot now. Are you stupid? The police will be here any minute to watch Rich's place again and you're out in the middle of the street causing a scene." Dylan says.

Stuart pulls the flap down and orders Casey into the back. He reluctantly goes in and Naz sits on the floor as Rich squeezes into the back.

"So where did you guys go?"

"We went to pay our respects to Jay." Dylan answers quite sternly as he looks at Rich and turns away.

"What? You guys went to the funeral?"

"Sort of. So where was it you were rushing off to then." Adam says.

"Well when I realised you guys had left I thought I would head off to a mates house. Where are you guys going now?" Rich says trying to change the subject.

Nobody answers and Rich starts to get a little paranoid.

"What's going on? What are you guys up to?...Stuart?" Rich says turning to face him for an answer.

Stuart looks back at him but shrugs his shoulders and then faces forward again.

"We're going to Bruce's house and we're going to make him tell the truth about killing Jay." Dylan says.

"I didn't think you were serious."

"Oh we're serious."

"I thought you needed his address."

"Yeah did you get it?"

"We've got it too." Naz blurts out.

"How did you get it?" Rich asks.

"We followed him from the funeral."

Adam turns quickly and stares at Naz but he doesn't know what's going on.

"What? What did I say?" Naz looks up from the floor of the car with a confused expression on his face.

"Can we see the address you got?" Adam says.
Rich hands it over and Adam looks at it and smiles then hands it over to Dylan.

"That's not Frank's or Bruce's address."

"What do you mean?"

"We followed them and that's not either of their addresses." Adam says.

"Let me see" Stuart says.

He reads it and looks at Rich.

"Who gave this to you?"

"Look I work for the council now. I got it easily from another worker." He says unconvincingly.

Adam looks at Stuart with a smug grin as if to say 'I told you so' but Stuart never saw Rich speaking to Frank and Bruce so he doesn't know what's going on either.

"Did you guys never think that they might not have been going home when you followed them?" Rich says.

"He's right you know. That could have been anybody's house they were going into."

Stuart flicks the piece of card, with the addresses on them, across the front of the car.

"So are you guys going straight there now?" Rich asks.

They all look at Adam including Stuart, who Rich now knows has no authority over what decisions are to be made. Dylan comments that he is hungry again.

"Dylan I'd love to know where you put all that food because you appear to be constantly hungry." Naz says.

"So how are we going to get food this time? You can't possibly be planning to go into a shop again." Stuart says.

"We can go to a take away. We have Rich with us now so he can go in and order for us." Dylan says as his eyes light up at the thought of burgers and chips.

"Good shout Dylan." Casey says from inside the boot.

18.

Smith is sitting back in his chair looking at the large board in front of him. The photos of the six faces of the boys stare back at him. Under each one contains information about their background and past crimes. To the right of the photos is a map of Dundee and the surrounding area. Shown on the map are small coloured pins to indicate each incident or citing of the boys movements. Smith gets out of his seat, stands in front of the map and stares at it for a long time. He tries to put himself in their situation and cannot figure out why they would leave the area. He has already been ridiculed for putting a stop to the road blocks as only an hour later they crashed through the barrier on the bridge and drove out of the city. He couldn't have planned it better if he tried. If he had gone ahead with the road blocks those boys might be in custody at this minute and he would never have the chance to flush out Billy. He knows if they are not picked up by tonight they will be back in the city. Nevin had suggested the possibility of the boys making some sort of appearance at the funeral but Smith discreetly put on extra officers in the hope of scaring the boys off.

"There's a call for you on line two." Nevin says as she enters his office.

"Who is it?"

"They wouldn't say."

Smith picks up the receiver and his partner leaves.

"Hello this is Detective Chief Inspector Smith speaking how can I help you?"

"Billy McGinty was picked up at Edinburgh train station today."

"How do you….?"

The line goes dead and Smith, although annoyed at being hung up on, smiles to himself at the information he has just received. He knows whose voice it was and the information will definitely cost him a large favour. He sits back in his chair still smiling and thinks that it is time to stop dragging his heals on the boys capture and to personally step up the search. If he can secretly keep track of the boys' whereabouts it will only be a matter of time before Billy catches up. Although this £10,000 reward does have him worried as every 'would be' hero is now on the lookout to get paid.

"Don't know if it's anything to go on but Rich Bryson went into his flat and left after a couple of minutes. Then he was seen getting into a car at the end of his street. Apparently it looked like it was full and it looked like a young boy in the drivers seat." Nevin says as she walks into Smith's office.

He is about to make a comment about her lack of knocking before entering first, but he lets it go.

"Did they follow it?"

"No they had specific instructions not to move but report anything unusual."

"And common sense didn't register that it could have been the boys? Did they get the registration by any chance?"

"They're running it through right now."

Smith turns and looks back at the map. He now starts to think that if those boys are still mobile this opens a whole new list of possibilities of where they could turn up and at the back of his mind, gives a much less chance of him capturing Billy.

***

Billy is driven through his old haunts and hardly recognises them. He has been away for so long and travelled to so many different countries that he has forgotten what this place looked like. The driver, a trusted friend of Kevin's, points out some of the old places that have been demolished to make way for new built homes and supermarkets. He looks out of the window and wishes he hadn't come back until they drive past a local newsagent's. There is a board out front with the latest headlines that remind him of exactly why he has returned. The driver takes him to The Pheasant, a rough old pub on the outskirts of the city that his old friend Kevin had taken over several years ago. He drives around to the side car park, parks the car, and they both walk around the back as the driver gives a light coded knock on the door. Billy is welcomed in with hugs and handshakes from Kevin and with warm smiles from a few old friends …all accept one.

The driver had informed Billy before entering the pub that Kevin is already onto one of their 'friends' for divulging information to Smith. After the pleasantries are out of the way Billy wastes no time in getting down to business. As they sit around the small table in the back of the pub Billy is brought up-to-date with the latest developments and is told a few truths that the newspapers would dare not print. Kevin is already on the trail of Williamson but he deliberately holds back a few of the specifics of their plans and he adds in some extra untrue details for the grass to report back to Smith.

The driver is given the address for Billy to hideout but this is changed as they walk out of the back door by means of a slip of paper secretly handed to the driver unaware of the preying eyes of the grass in their company.

***

Topher drives onto the main road opposite the takeaway shop and is unaware of the unmarked police car that has picked up their trail only minutes before. As they sit in the car giving Rich their orders of what food they want Adam pulls out a small role of cash from his pocket. He peels off several notes and hands them to Rich to pay for the order. He was unaware that it was taken from his secret stash the minute he left his flat to attend the funeral.

"Where did you get that money from Adam?" Dylan asks.

Adam doesn't answer but winks and smiles. Dylan shakes his head and smiles back.

Rich leaves the car and walks into the takeaway shop clocking the phone on the wall immediately. He makes the order at the till, pays the cashier and checks the change before putting it into his pocket. He looks up as he turns around and has a clear view of the car across the street where the boys are sitting. He looks over to the payphone and then back out of the window at the car. He walks over to the other side of the shop where a large pillar blocks his view. He wanders over to the phone and looks out the window again. He can't see the car from this angle either and he quickly thinks if he can't see them then they can't see him. He pulls out some of the change from his pocket and lifts the receiver off the phone. He can feel his heart beating faster as he dials the number. Without even saying his name he passes on information and walks back to the counter again. He glances out of the window at the boys in the car. His order is ready and he leaves the shop with a large bag.

"Did you get everything?" Adam says as he walks up behind him.

Rich's body shudders with fright as he turns to see Adam.

"Oh eh yeah, I got everything. Where have you been?"

"I had to pee." Adam says with a smug look on his face.

They walk back to the car where Rich watches the boys eat like they haven't eaten in days.

Adam gives Dylan a sly wink to confirm what he has seen.

***

Smith has radio contact with his two officers who are only metres away watching their every move. He gives them specific instructions to keep their distance and not to do anything to jeopardise their position. Smith puts out a call for all patrols to be on standby and is about to rush out of the station when he receives an urgent call. It's his informant again, who passes on the address of where Billy is hiding out. Smith suddenly slows down as he contemplates the situation. He wants to capture Billy so badly but he can't take the risk of being thrown off the case if Billy isn't there. He lets it go and for the time being he decides to catch up with the tail on the boys.

***

During the journey to Bruce's Adam notices the same car passes them twice. The driver and passenger look straight ahead as if not to arouse suspicion, which for Adam, does exactly that. Adam tells Topher to pull in to the side of the road and they wait patiently to allow several cars to pass them. The officers tailing them radio Smith in a panic, thinking they've lost them. Smith looks at his map and thinks about the direction the boys are travelling and reassures his officers of where the boys are going to.

He calls for all units to cover every exit within a half a mile radius of Bruce's address.

***

"We've got them, they're going nowhere now" says one of the lowlife's to his buddy as they sit in their rusted car listening to their scanner which has been illegally tuned into the police frequency. The driver starts the car and speeds off in the hope of beating the police to one of the exit points before a road block is set up. The passenger checks the two weapons they intend to use to capture the boys. One, a sawn off shotgun which has already been used in a failed attempted robbery in the past month. The other is an automatic pistol which was purchased down south only hours after the reward was announced.

***

In the back of the Pheasant pub, Billy and his friends sit patiently around a small table also listening to an illegally tuned scanner. As soon as Bruce's address is announced over the scanner Billy is anxious to make a move but is advised to wait.

***

The boys park a few hundred yards from Bruce's house and Adam can sense that something is not right. It's still early evening and not a single car has passed on the busy road opposite them. He also notices Rich acting a little strange. He wanted to ask him about the phone call he made from the takeaway but he can sense now what it was about.
The boys step out of the car and as Adam opens the boot to allow Casey to climb out he makes eye contact with Dylan who gives him the nod and a lift of the eyebrows in the direction of Rich. Adam thinks that for someone who looks and acts unintelligent he's clicked on to Rich quicker than the rest of the other boys. Adam tells Topher to stay with the car and to leave the engine running. Unbeknown to the boys, as they make their way towards the back of the row of houses where Bruce lives, they are being watched in the darkness by police officers, the armed lowlifes and also the occupants of Bruce's house who have now gathered together after the unexpected phone call and are now ready and waiting. Adam whispers out loudly as he counts down the number of houses and intentionally points out the wrong one as Bruce's. The boys gather at the back gate to Bruce's garden as Adam informs them of his plan.

"Me and Dylan will go in through this gate to his back door. Stuart and Rich, you guys go in through the neighbour's gate and wait there. Casey and Naz, you guys go into the other neighbour's gate and do the same."

"Why?" Stuart says feeling confused but relieved that he is not going in after Bruce.

"Because, if he manages to escape and does a runner there will be someone at either side to catch him" Adam replies.

"What do we do when we catch him?" Rich asks.

"The same as he did to Jay." Casey mumbles.

"Casey." Adam says nudging him to be quiet.

"But I thought we were just going to capture him and force him to tell the truth." Rich says.

"We are, we are." Adam says giving Casey a stern look that he can just make out in the dark.

Stuart and Rich make their way over to the neighbour's fence and watch as Adam and Dylan enter through the back gate. They do the same and are too busy watching next door to notice two dark figures creeping up behind them. The two lowlifes make their move and pounce on Stuart and Rich. The two boys shout for help as they struggle to free themselves. Casey and Naz, who are oblivious to what is really going on, begin climbing the fence to go and help them only to be held back by Dylan.

"Don't be stupid, it's a set up." Adam whispers.

The boys crouch down in the darkness and watch as several men come charging out of the house, with Bruce in the front armed with a large stick and a torch he runs straight towards the lowlifes as they struggle with the boys. A shot is fired from the lowlife's pistol and the light from the torch falls as Bruce hit's the deck. The rest of the men back off quickly and try to run and hide. Stuart manages to free himself and also makes a run for it. Another shot is fired and the boys watch through the darkness as the shadow of their friend falls to the ground in front of them. The loud shots from the pistol alert the police who swoop into action. The first policeman on the scene shines his torch on Stuart's still, blood soaked body. He works his way up with the torch to see the other lowlife with his arm around Rich's neck and a sawn off shotgun pointed under his chin. As the police are unarmed a call is made to headquarters to dispense the armed response unit immediately. The police on the scene try to calm the situation but keep their distance. Within minutes the whole place is turned into chaos as nosy neighbours come out of their homes and kids out playing come running from streets to investigate the commotion. The two lowlifes are surrounded by police and Smith talks to the men to try and stall them as the armed police get themselves set up. Adam uses the disruption to make his getaway. He tugs on the other boys' arms and leads the way back out to the street. They blend in with the crowds that have gathered and enjoy listening and adding to the comments being made about them as they stand with their arms folded smiling smugly to each other. They discreetly make their way up the street towards the car and at first think that they have been caught as the armed response unit van speeds up to them blocking their path. Adam turns to look for another getaway when the police van's horn sounds and the boys look on in shock as they see Topher's wide eyes and cheeky grin staring at them from behind the steering wheel of the police van. The boys jump in and take off up the street.

"Where's Stuart and Rich?" Topher says.

"They're gone." Adam says as he looks around at the others.

"Gone. What do you mean they're gone?"

"They're just gone. Okay." Dylan says quietly.

"Oh oh." Topher says.

"What?" Adam says.

"Up ahead. Look."

Not far in front of them is a road block and Topher starts to slow down.

"What are you doing?"

"Away to turn around, we'll have to find another way out."

"Put the foot down."

"But…"

Adam pushes and fiddles around with buttons and switches until the blue lights start to flash.

"Go for it." Adam shouts.

Topher smiles as he slams his foot on the accelerator and puts the pedal to the floor. As the van speeds up the two patrol cars blocking the road begin to separate. Topher stares ahead as he concentrates on the gap and misses each car by inches on either side. The boys howl and gesture as they look back at the police who are oblivious to who has just passed them.

The two lowlifes take Rich as their hostage to escape back to their rusty car. They are given space to drive off as the armed police search unsuccessfully to find their vehicle. They scramble into patrol cars to continue their pursuit which ends only several miles from the scene as the lowlife's car runs out of petrol. Before they step out of the car they are surrounded by police marksmen. On the instructions of the police the lowlifes drop their weapons and lie on the floor. Rich is arrested along with the men as he is mistaken for one of the gang of boys they are looking for.

The boys laugh as they listen to the police radio with the news about the arrests but their smiles soon drop from their faces when other news comes in that one of the gang is pronounced dead at the scene.

"Guys, what the hell happened back there." Topher says.

"Rich set us up." Dylan says.

"How do you know that?"

"I saw him making a phone call at the take-away place when he went in to buy our food."

"So now they're just going to shoot us." Casey says.

"I don't know. I don't think those guys that shot Stuart had anything to do with Frank or Bruce."

A message comes over the police radio from Smith who has just been informed about the boys' getaway.

He appeals to the boys that if they are listening to get in touch with him immediately.

"Is anyone going to answer that?" Naz says.

"I'm not. Unless you want to say hello." Adam says offering Naz the receiver.

Dylan reaches over and grabs it, stretching the cord to the limit as he sits farthest away.

"I didn't murder my uncle."

The rest of the boys sit in silence and Topher pulls over to the side of the road.

"Keep driving Topher. I think they can track us quicker if we stop." Adam says.

"I take it this is Dylan I'm talking to." Smith says.

"I'm not talking to you. I'm telling you. It was self-defence. He picked up the knife and tried to stab me. We struggled and fell to the floor. When I got up the knife was in him. Check the finger prints on the handle. I didn't even touch it."

"I'll do that Dylan. In the mean time why don't you boys meet me and we can talk about this. I could come and meet you on my own. One of your friends is already dead. We don't want anymore of you boys hurt…"

Dylan lets the receiver go and it springs back towards the radio.

"Just turn it off." Dylan mumbles.
Smith is half way through another little speech to the boys when Adam switches it off.

19.

Although Billy appears calm as he hears about the lowlifes failed escape coming through the scanner his palms have been sweating constantly. As he sits in the front with Kevin with his other two friends in the back they listen intently waiting for an opportunity to help out the boys without putting themselves at risk. With Billy's friends connections the two lowlifes would not last long in prison and within a day they will be volunteering to be kept in solitary. They have already discussed the possibility of going after The Program's wardens and by any means necessary finding out the truth about what happened, but this was deemed a high risk.

Information comes through the scanner that the boys have dumped the van in a car park on the edge of the city. Kevin circles past the car park and within minutes the place is swarming with blue lights. They know that the boys would have been long gone, too long even for the dogs to pick up their scent. A message is put out to Smith that a Glock 17 police issue revolver is missing from its casing. There is no reply from Smith. One of Kevin's friends receives a message on his pager. They pull over at a phone box and make a call. The friend on the other line informs him of the raid on the fake hideout as he watches from across the street. This now confirms that Smith is definitely onto one of their associates.

"If there was a raid planned why wasn't it on the scanner?" Billy's friend says from the back of the car.

"Smith is smarter than you think. He'll have used a different frequency. He knows we are listening. That's why he's not bothered about us hearing the information about the boys because he wants us to know. Hoping we'll turn up." Kevin says.

***

After dumping the van. Topher leads the way in search of another form of transport. As they walk towards a busy street with rows of cars Dylan keeps talking about Stuart being shot and killed. As much as the rest of the boys feel bad for what happened Dylan is making it worse.

"But I mean that could have easily been any one of us."

"Look Dylan. We know. Will you please just stop going on about it." Casey says.

"But it's just that if that's what the rest of us are looking at then theirs something I have to do guys."

"What? Oh don't tell me you're still a virgin Dylan?"

"No. It's nothing to do with that."

"Well what's wrong? Spit it out."

"Adam?" Dylan pleads.

Adam knows exactly what's on Dylan's mind…Sarah.

"Dylan I promise we'll go and see her tomorrow but right now if Topher hurries up and finds us a car then I may have a good place for us to hide out tonight. Hot food and a warm place to sleep." Adam says.

"Where?" Topher asks.

"Car, now." Adam demands as he points up the street. After a few attempts Topher breaks the steering lock on a fairly new car and the boys are again travelling in luxury.

"So what's the story Dylan? Who is it you're wanting to go and see?" Naz asks.

"It's just someone I know. I just want to say thanks and the way it's going for us…probably goodbye."

"Don't say that Dylan. You're starting to get us depressed."

Adam directs Topher onto the dual carriageway and instructs him to turn off when he sees a familiar name on the sign post. Jay had taken him here not long after he had joined the program. Kathy had taken a liking to Jay the moment she met him and he always went out of his way to make sure Adam could visit her whenever possible. There was a small car park to the rear of the building, out of sight from passers-by.

"So what's this place?" Naz asks.

"It's sheltered housing. My old foster mother lives here. We'll be safe for tonight."

"But I thought you hated your foster family."

"It's a different one. Come on let's go."

Adam puts the safety catch on the revolver and puts it down the front of his trousers. He creeps quietly into the building with the boys close behind him. After knocking lightly on her door a low voice answers.

"Who is it?"

"It's me. It's Adam."

The door opens and Kathy looks out at the five boys' face's who appear tired, gaunt and in need of a good scrub.

"Hurry up. Get in before someone sees you." Kathy says.

The other boys look at each other and smile. Dylan goes straight to the T.V. and sits down. The rest of the boys follow.

"I take it you boys are hungry."

They all turn and nod at Kathy.

"Well make yourselves at home and go get yourselves cleaned up I'll make you something to eat."

"Thanks Kathy." They all say.

Adam follows Kathy into the kitchen to give her a hand and shuts the door behind him.

"We didn't do it Kathy."

"Kathy turns and hugs him

"I know son."

Adam feels a lump in his throat as he hasn't heard Kathy call him that since he lived with her and Old Charlie. For a few seconds his mind is transported back to when he was a small boy and they made him feel safe in their company.

They hear a knock on the kitchen door and release from each other.

"Are you needing a hand with anything?" Dylan asks as he enters.

"No. It's okay Dylan we'll be fine."

Dylan goes back into the living room and joins the other boys who are sitting eagerly around the T.V. waiting on the news to come on. Kathy serves up the boys some hot soup and watches with a smile as they devour a whole loaf of bread between them. Later as they tuck into a plate of sausage chips and beans the news eventually comes on. The reporter confirms that one of the gang has been shot and killed by vigilantes out to collect the reward money. One of the Security Wardens Bruce Harrington from The Program has also been shot and is in intensive care in Ninewells hospital under police guard. She goes onto say that two men have been arrested after a police chase. They believed that they had taken one of the gang members hostage and their getaway car ran out of petrol.

The boys see the funny side of this and even Kathy breaks out into a smile. Rich's face is shown on the screen and Casey shouts. "Traitor."

"Unknown to the two men the suspected member of

the gang was a former resident of The Program. He has also been arrested on suspicion of helping the gang in attempting to murder the former Warden who was one of the key witnesses in the gang's brutal murder of Jason Fallon. Due to the involvement of firearms the police have now stepped up their search and deployed armed officers to various parts of the city."

Dylan reaches over and changes the channel. "I hate the way they portray us to be a gang."

"What do you think we should do Kathy?" Adam says.

"Well the last thing I want is for any of you boys to get hurt. You could leave the country. I could get in touch with one of Charlie's old friends. His son is a long distance lorry driver. He could maybe take you over to France or somewhere."

"Yeah, France. I could live in France. Yeah that sounds good to me. " Casey says trying to convince himself. The rest of the boys don't answer as they contemplate the option laid out for them.

"You boys had best be getting some rest anyway. If you want I'll make a call in the morning and see what he says. There are spare blankets and pillows in the cupboard in the hall. You'll just have to make room on the floor."

"That's okay Kathy it's probably one of the comfier places we've had to sleep in a while." Dylan says.

"Good night boys."

"Good night Kathy." The boys say as she disappears into her room.

The boys try to make themselves comfortable on the floor.

"So what do you think Adam? Do you think France is a good idea?" Casey says.

"And let Frank and Bruce go free after what they did to Jay."

"Adam we're not going to get near them now. Bruce has guards around his hospital room you heard it yourself. Not to mention the armed police all over the city who I'll bet are just waiting for the chance to take us out. I think we should take the France option."

"For once I think we agree on something." Naz says.

"Well I'm staying. I'm going to stay until the job is done." Adam says.

"Why Adam? You know anything you do is not going to bring Jay back."

"Look guys. Before Jay put me on this program I had nothing. My life was destined to be spent locked up. We could take a chance and go to France but what if we get caught and don't make it then all of this will be for nothing. You know we have to finish it for Jay…and Stuart. I'm staying and I'm going to see it through."

"Me too." Topher says.

"Me too. But first I've got to do something." Dylan says nodding over at Adam.

"We'll go in the morning Dylan. What about you two?"

"Naz looks at Casey and thinks for a minute. You're right Adam. We should see it through, for Jay." He says.
Casey looks at Naz and nods. As he turns back to the others he nods again and smiles.

"We see it through." Adam says.

Naz thought he had woken first until he heard someone in the bathroom. He looked around the floor. It must be Dylan he thought. He went into the kitchen and poured himself a glass of water. On his return the bathroom door opened and Kathy appeared. Naz stood in the doorway looking confused.

"Are you okay?" Kathy asks.

"Eh'm. Yeah I thought it was Dylan in the toilet. That's all."

The other boys waken up when they hear voices.

"What's wrong?" Adam asks.

"I'm just wondering where Dylan is?"

"What do you mean?"

"Well. He's not here"

"Are you sure?"

"Adam. He's gone."

"But why would he leave? Where would he go?" Kathy asks.

"I have a pretty good idea. What time is it?"

"8.30"

"Come on guys. We'll have to hurry."

"Where to?"

"I'll tell you on the way. Let's go."

The boys run to the car and take off in search of Sarah's school. After a few wrong turns Topher eventually finds it. He drives slowly up and down the narrow streets surrounding the school as they frantically look for Dylan.

"What will we do if we can't find him?" Naz asks.

"Go back to Kathy's and wait for him there I guess."

"Wait. I think I saw him. Stop" Casey says.

"Where?" Topher says.

"Over there by the trees just up from the main gate."

"What's he doing?"

"Nothing. He's just standing there."

"He's waiting on Sarah." Adam says.

"What do we do? If we go and get him we could all be seen."

"Topher pull over and park on the pavement off the main road and keep it running. We'll just watch and see what happens."

The boys watch from a short distance as Dylan waits impatiently, inspecting every car that pulls up and every person who walks by. At 8.50 Dylan is about to give up hope when a car pulls up close to the entrance and a small, pretty, innocent looking girl steps out. Dylan's eyes light up but he tries to stay calm and wait until her father drives off but she is about to enter the school and he knows this is his only chance.

"Sarah." He shouts in a low voice.
She keeps walking.
"Sarah." He shouts louder.
She turns her head to see a tall dark figure hiding in the trees. She knows his voice and without thinking she runs to him."

"No. No go back. You're dad will see me."
She ignores him and keeps running. She drops her bag on the ground and throws her arms around him.

"I missed you Dylan."
"I just came to explain. I didn't want you to think…"
"It's okay. I know you would never do that."

Dylan smiles to himself as he drapes his arms around her. His moment of happiness is short lived as Sarah's dad grabs him from behind and tackles him to the ground. Dylan doesn't resist and keeps looking at Sarah and smiling. Adam, Casey and Naz run to help him. Dylan is now on his feet with both arms locked behind his back. Sarah is crying and shouting at her father to let him go but Dylan is reassuring her that it's going to be okay.

"Let him go." Adam shouts.

"It's okay Adam. Just leave me. I'm ready to face them and tell the truth."

Sarah's father looks around at the other boys and then at his daughter. Adam lifts up his shirt to reveal the revolver and looks at Dylan. He has no intension of using it but hopes it will scare Sarah's father into letting Dylan go. Dylan shakes his head and smiles. During the commotion other teachers and parents are alerted and come running towards them. Adam backs away.

"Dad please. Don't do this." Sarah pleads with her father.

He releases Dylan's arms and Sarah steps forward. Dylan puts his arms around her.

"Dylan come on. We've got to go." Adam shouts.

Dylan ignores him.

The other teachers are getting close and Sarah's dad taps him on the shoulder.

"I think you had better go now son before they get here." Dylan looks around at him and smiles. He kisses Sarah on the forehead and then runs off to catch the other boys. The teachers and parents stop running when they reach Sarah and her dad.

"Did they hurt you?" One of them says.

"No. We're fine." Sarah says as she looks at her dad and they both smile.

"What the hell are you playing at Dylan? You could have got us all caught." Casey says as Topher speeds off. Dylan doesn't answer but the boys all look at him and laugh as he sits in the back of the car with a large satisfied smile.

20.

Kathy hears a sharp knock on the door and she immediately pictures the police standing there ready to question her. As she opens the door she has answers already prepared in her head. She stands looking at someone who appears to be familiar but can't quite place him.

"Hi. Kathy." The stranger says and smiles.

As soon as she hears his voice she realises who he is.

"You look just like your father."

"Well I am Billy's kid."

"You certainly are."

"What the hell happened Kathy."

"You had better come in and sit down."

Billy goes to walk in the door.

"Oh by the way. You've just missed your brother, they stayed here last night."

***

The boys find themselves at the crematorium as they felt they never had the chance to say a proper goodbye to Jay. Apart from some old lady walking around, the place is deserted so early in the morning. The police and reporters will be at Sarah's school probably listening to fabricated stories of what happened with Dylan.

They find Jay's urn next to a small plaque and the boys sit down in a semi circle on the damp grass and stare at it.

"It's not what I was expecting." Naz says.
"Me neither." Adam says.
"That's so sad, after everything he did for other people.
You would think they would have given him a suitable headstone."
"You don't get headstones when you get cremated."
"Why?"
"I don't know. I think some people bury the ashes with other relatives who are already buried."
"What do you think Jay would say if he saw us here right now?" Dylan says.
"He would probably tell us to hand ourselves in." Topher says.
"Maybe. But he wouldn't want us to be convicted for his murder and he also wouldn't want Frank getting away with it. No. I think he would be proud of us for sticking together and getting as far as we have." Adam says.
Dylan nods at this and smiles as he thinks about Jay looking down on them.
"So what's the plan now? What's next?" Naz asks.
There is a long silence as the boys think to themselves. Most are waiting on Adam making a decision but Dylan steps in.
"I think we should finish it." Dylan says.
"What do you mean? Naz asks.
"You know what I'm saying. We can't let him get away with it. We have nothing to lose. Let's do this for Jay."
Adam smiles. He takes the revolver out of his waist band and holds it out in front of him over Jay's grave with his palm facing down. His smile drops and he says "For Jay."
Dylan puts his palm on top and smiles. "For Jay."
Topher does the same. Then Casey. The rest of the boys look at Naz. He looks at the plaque and then back at the

boys. He smiles and slaps his hand on top of the others.

"I say we make an oath right here. Right now. That if anything happens to any one of us the others promise to continue until Frank and Bruce and anyone else responsible are brought down in any way that they can be." Adam says. The boys all make their promise.

***

After saying goodbye to Kathy. Billy is driven by Kevin to the address that Kathy gave him. One he vaguely remembers after posting several letters there in the past. The house is located in a respectable area with tidy gardens and expensive cars. Kevin waits in the car while Billy walks up the path to the front door. He thought about knocking but decided that would attract more attention. He tries the door, It's open. The hallway is immaculate and smells like a hospital. He peers into the living room where a large man is sat in a chair reading his paper. Billy casually walks in and sits opposite him.

"What the...?"

"Shh." Billy says as he puts his finger to his lips. "Do you know who I am?"

"I have no idea." The man says quite smugly.

After moving the paper Billy clocks the man's massive gut. In a sudden movement Billy stands up and in a downward motion he punches his fist into the man's gut. The man bolts forward in his seat clutching his stomach while coughing and spluttering. Billy casually sits back down.

"Now, just so that I know I have the right person. I'll ask again. Do you know who I am?"

The man looks up with a face of sheer agony and nods.

"Good. That will save me the trouble in explaining why

I'm here. I take it you are Harry?"
Billy pulls out a small revolver and places it on his lap.

"Look. I never meant Adam any harm. We took good care of him. You know how boys are, he was a bit of a handful. So we had to get strict with him."

"Strict with him?" Billy says and smiles to himself.

He then reaches forward and smacks him in the head with the side of the revolver.

"Now. What did you do with those letters?"

"What letters?"

Billy reaches forward and smacks him in the head with the revolver again. Harry puts his hands up to his head to protect himself from more blows so Billy throws another punch down to his gut. He casually sits back down and waits on him recovering.

"Okay you have one last chance. What did you do with the letters?"

"I don't know what letters you're talking about."

Billy stands up again but before he hits out he hears footsteps and as the living room door opens Billy points the revolver. Linda enters.

"Here." She says holding out her hand with several opened envelopes.

Billy takes them and quickly scans the writing to confirm it's his letters. He looks up and puts the revolver back in his pocket along with the letters. He looks down at Harry and pictures in his head this bullying beast of a man slapping around little Adam. Then in a total rage he lets loose with a barrage of punches to his face and gut. Linda screams and tries to pull him off but Billy pushes her away. Billy eventually stops and he looks down at his knuckles which are swollen and bloody. Harry is slouched in the chair, knocked out. Linda is sitting on the floor crying.

"Now, just so that you know, If anything happens to my little brother I'm going to come back here and finish him off."

He walks out of the house and Kevin is still waiting in the car with the engine running. He doesn't bat an eyelid at the blood on Billy's hands as he's seen this many times in his line of work.

"Why didn't you use the gun?"

"I needed to let off some steam."

"Feel better now."

"Uh huh."

Kevin smiles and drives off.

***

Smith receives an urgent call by his partner to an assault in a house on the edge of the city. When he arrives on the scene a large man whose face is unrecognisable due to the amount of swelling is being helped into an ambulance.

"You're not going to believe this one." Nevin says.

"The boys never done this, surely."

"No, it was the older brother of one of the boys. You're very own Billy the kid."

Smith smirks. "Who are they?"

"Adam's old foster family. I just took a statement from the mother. She says Billy came looking for some letters that he had sent to Adam in the past but they hadn't ever bothered passing them on to him."

Smith looks away and thinks to himself.

"He's not seen his brother in over ten years. They obviously lost touch when Adam was with that family and he's looking for the letters to prove that he tried to keep contact. Billy must be getting ready to make his move to help them. Come on. We've got to move. I have a few ideas.

***

Adam's plan was to go back to Kathy's and hide out until dark but on approaching the sheltered housing complex they
spot officers in an unmarked police car parked not far from the main entrance.

"So what do we do now?" Topher asks.

"I don't know. Just drive." Adam says.

Where to?"

"I don't know. Anywhere. Just drive until we can think of someplace to go."

"That's not a good idea Adam. There are road blocks all over the city now and spot checks. Not to mention this car, which has probably been reported stolen by now"

"Topher's right Adam. We need to hide out until tonight." Dylan says.

"I think I know a place." Naz says.

"It's not one of those churches where you have to take off your shoes, kneel down and pray to some God is it?" Casey says.

"It's a mosque, not a church and they pray to Allah not God."

"Hey, if it's warm and safe then I'm up for it." Topher says.

"Stop the car Topher." Adam says.

"Why?"

"Just stop."

Adam gets out.

"Naz. You're up front. Give Topher directions." Adam says as he gets in the back.

"Aww guys. You're not serious about going there." Casey says.

"You heard him. It's warm and it's safe. If you have any other suggestions then let us hear them."

"Why didn't you mention this place before Naz." Dylan says.

"I never really thought about it. Remember my family hasn't spoken to me since I was sent to the Institution."

"Then who was it that came to visit you all those times?"

"My oldest brother. None of the family knew he came to visit me or he would have been made an outsider the same as me."

Naz directed Topher to an area in Dundee that none of the other boys have ever been to or even knew existed.

"Wow look at the size of these houses, or are they hotels?" Dylan says.

"No, they're houses. Pull up here Topher. You guys wait here while I go and check it out."

Naz walks down the street and looks up at some of his old friends' houses from when he was growing up. He pictures them in his mind and thinks about what they would be doing right now. He also wonders what they and their families will think of him after all this. Then he thinks about what his own family and what they will think of him. He reaches the back wall that surrounds the mosque and looks up at the building wishing he could turn back time to before all this started. He longs for the days when he was close to his family. He checks the back door and there is a small padlock on it. He feels along the top ledge and finds the key. After all those years they still keep it in the same place. There was never any need for much security at the mosque as there is nothing of any value in the place. The back door leads to a small room with no windows and Naz puts his hand in to feel for the light switch. He looks around the place. There are many chairs scattered around and in the middle is an old coffee table. On the edge of the table is an envelope with Naz's name written on it in large graffiti style writing. He knows the style. It's his brothers. He steps into the room and tears it open.

"Hey Naz, if you are reading this I guess you've not been caught yet and you're obviously running out of places to go. I know the family has washed their hands of you. Even more so now. But we (you're brothers) know you're not capable of murder. We have managed to scrape together some money (without father knowing) and have arranged transport back to India where you will be looked after and be able to have a fresh start in life. There is a contact number for you to call and they will sort you out with a fake passport and go over the fine details. Take care and we'll come visit you once you're settled."

Naz sits down and stares at the letter. He knows his brothers must have gone to a lot of trouble to do this for him and it must have been hard to keep it all from his father. He feels torn between his friends and his family and must make a decision about what is best for him. He walks back to the car and tells the others to follow him.

"I'm not away to go into a mosque." Casey says. Topher takes the key out of the car.

"Well you can stay here and freeze." He says as he gets out of the car and walks with Naz. The others do the same as Casey keeps sitting.

"Come on Casey. Don't be so stupid." Dylan says.
Casey gets out of the car and slams the door shut. He walks slowly on, trailing behind them.
They enter the small room and find a seat. Casey stays standing.

"Casey will you sit down. We know you don't want to be here but it's only for a few hours until it gets dark." Adam says.

Casey sits down and makes a large sigh.
Adam takes the revolver out of his trousers and puts it on the coffee table. The rest of the boys stare at it. Topher picks it up and starts aiming it around the room pretending to shoot random objects.

"If we get the chance can I shoot Frank?"

"You can shoot both of them if you want." Adam says.

"Cool."

"What about me I want to shoot one of them." Casey says taking the revolver from Topher.

"Look we'll see what happens guys, okay."

"What is it with you guys? We are on the run for murder, trying to prove that we are innocent and all you are thinking about is who gets to kill who." Naz says.
Topher and Casey look at each other and smile before they both say "Yeah."

Naz sits and stares at the two of them and then at the revolver as they pass it between them. He has visions of being shot and tries to imagine what it would feel like. The revolver is put back onto the coffee table and he watches and waits as all the boys eventually drift off to sleep.
Upon wakening only a few hours later they notice Naz is gone. Adam gets up out of the chair and opens the door into the main area of the mosque. It's dark and empty. He shouts out for Naz but there is not answer.

"Adam I think you had better look at this."
Adam takes the letter from Dylan and reads it.

"He's gone?"

Dylan nods.

"What do you mean he's gone?" Casey says grabbing the letter.

"It says something about a number to call."

"Yeah he's torn it off and left the notes so that we know he's not coming back."

"Great. So what do we do now Adam?" Dylan says.

"We do what we set out to do. We made an oath remember."

Topher opens the door to the room. "It's dark you guys." Adam picks up the revolver and puts it back in his waist band.

"Right, let's get this over with."

21.

Naz had to call the number quite a few times before he got an answer. When he did get through the person on the other line asked his whereabouts and told him to wait there and that someone would pick him up. Naz was still unsure if what he was doing was the right thing. He walked away and returned several times as he waited. In the end he decided to stay.

He was taken to a warehouse full of pallets of grocery supplies and was led into an office out the back. His oldest brother was waiting there. Without saying a word they both hugged each other.

"It's good to see you Naz." He says as they break off. They sit down and talk for a while and Naz explains what really happened to Jay.

"So where are the rest of the boys now."

"I don't know I left them in the room at the back of the mosque. But there plan is to go after Frank and Bruce. Adam has a gun."

"Look Naz. There's someone who needs to talk to you."

"Who?"

"He's a detective, but he's okay. It's him that's helped me arrange your escape. But he just needs some information from you."

"Like what?"

Naz's brother leaves the room and returns moments later with Detective Chief Inspector Smith. Naz stands up and backs away from him.

"Calm down Naz. I'm not here to arrest you. Sit down."
Naz stays standing.

"Sit down." Smith demands.

"Come on Naz. Just sit down and talk to the detective then we can get you out of here."

Naz reluctantly sits down opposite Smith who has his notebook ready.

"Right where are the rest of the boys?"

"I don't know. When I left them they were sleeping but they'll have left now."

"Left to go where?"

Naz clams up. Smith knows they'll be heading for Frank but he is trying to get Naz talking to find out what he really wants to know.

"Did you or any of the other boys take a revolver from the van you used as a getaway."

"Naz shakes his head."

"Look Naz. If you care about you're friends you'll tell me what I need to know. It's for there own good."

Naz nods.

"Who took it?"

"Adam."

"Does he still have it?"

Naz nods again.

"What is he planning on doing with it?"

"Going after Frank and Bruce for killing Jay."

"Well going after Bruce may be a waste of time because I don't think he's going to make it anyway."

"Good." Naz says.

"What about Jack? Who killed Jack?"

"He was already dead when we got there. I swear, we only went there to ask him for help."

"It's okay. I believe you."

"Well if you believe me. Why haven't you arrested them then?"

"Has Adam had any contact with his brother Billy?"

"No. Why?"

"He's wanted for questioning and we are trying to track him down. We have information that he has came back into the country to help Adam. Are you sure Adam has had no contact with him."

"I'm sure. Adam doesn't even like to talk about him."

"What about any of Billy's friends? Have they contacted or tried to contact Adam?"

"No, not that I know of."

Smith starts to put his notepad away.

"So are you going to arrest Frank and Bruce?"

"Eventually, but right now we need them as bait for Adam's brother and we need Adam as bait for his brother." Smith says with a large smug grin on his face.

He gets up to leave and turns back, still grinning he says "Oh and I hope you have a safe journey back to India." Naz's brother gives him the thumbs up and smiles but Naz doesn't return his enthusiasm. He sits in silence as it sinks in exactly what's going on. Smith has been using him and the rest of the boys to try and capture Adam's brother. Once they have him they will go 'all out' to catch his friends. Now that Adam is armed they will shoot to kill. It also makes him realise that if Smith can go to these lengths to catch Adam's brother from that many years ago there is no way he is ever going to let him leave. He has to get back to the boys and warn Adam that the whole thing is a trap.

***

Billy and his friends are sitting around a table waiting on the news when a message comes over the receiver that the boys are on their way to Frank's. They are armed and dangerous and not to approach them.

"It's time to make our move Billy." Kevin says.

"Okay call the grass. Let him know what's happening. Tell him to stay there and we'll pick him up on the way. That should give him enough time to inform Smith."

Billy picks up the shotgun from the table and starts to load it. There is another automatic revolver still on the table and Kevin takes out a small box of rounds and begins loading it.

"Are those blanks?" Billy asks.

"Sure are. This weapon is for our little talkative friend to use." Kevin says smiling.

After the grass receives the phone call he hangs up and within seconds he is back on it dialing Smith's number.

"Smith?"

"This is D.C.I Smith."

"Billy's making his move tonight."

"This had better be for real. After the last fiasco with the hideout your skating on thin ice my friend."

'You're skating on thin ice'. What is he all about? I think he's watched too many old detective movies the grass thinks to himself before answering.

"It's real. I'm being picked up to go with them."

***

A car pulls up several streets away and police surveillance calls over the radio to confirm it's them. Smith only has to make the order and those boys would be in custody in a matter of minutes but he hesitates. He wants Billy.

"Sir. You'll be putting Frank's life in danger if you let those boys go any further. Our men can take them now while they are all together." Nevin says.

"They are not altogether. There's more to come."

"What do you mean?"

"I have information that Billy McGinty is on his way here to help them."

"Excuse me Sir, but our job is to make sure that those boys or anyone else for that matter don't come to any harm. Not for you to go around putting them at risk to end a grudge you've had from years ago."

"Excuse me detective but who do you think you are talking to. I give the orders here. No one is going to be put at risk. You know yourself those boys aren't murderers and there is no way they will walk in there and shoot Frank."

"Maybe. But what about his brother?
Smith thinks for few seconds. "We wait." He says
quite abruptly.

"Fine. But if this all blows up. You're taking the blame."
Smith shrugs his shoulders and looks back out onto
the street.

Adam checks the revolver before leaving the car. He takes the safety catch off and puts if back in his waistband. The four boys walk nervously down the street towards Frank's house. Unaware they are being watched from every possible direction.

"Which way Adam?" Casey says.

"What do you mean?"

"Back or front?"
Adam thinks for a second.

"The front. We're going straight through the front door. It's time to finish this once and for all."
Adam's enthusiasm gives the rest of the boys'

Youngsters 186

encouragement with Casey and Topher putting an extra few inches on their swagger and a lift in their step. They reach Frank's gate and look up the path to his door. Adam takes the gun out of his waistband and turns to the others. "You guys ready?"
The boys nod.

Adam turns and sprints towards the door. He charges it with his shoulder and it bursts open. He walks into the living room to find Frank getting to his feet.

"What the…?"

"Hello Frank." Adam says pointing the revolver at him. Frank puts his hands up and the rest of the boys appear at Adam's side.

"Get on your knees."

Frank goes to step forward and Adam clicks back the leaver. "Knees." he says staring wildly into Frank's eyes. Frank drops to his knees and Adam puts the revolver to his temple.

"Don't do it Adam." A familiar voice says.

Adam and the rest of the boys turn to see five armed men bursting through from the back door.

"It's me Adam. It's Billy."

Adam lowers the revolver.

"What…Wh?"

"This is Detective Chief Inspector Smith. The house is completely surrounded. Put your weapons down and come out with your hands in the air."

Smith announces over a loud speaker from the front of the house.

"Billy. What…?" Adam is still shocked.

"We'll talk later Adam. Right now I think we have other things to sort out."

"We only came here to get him." Adam says angrily

pointing the revolver back at Frank's head.

"If you do that you will become exactly what they are writing about you in the papers - a murderer. Is that what you want to be known as?"

"What's the difference? They're never going to believe us now anyway."

Through the window a sharp shooter informs Smith he has the shot on Adam. He gives the signal to fire. Billy reaches over to take the revolver from Adam and a shot is fired. Adam is caught on his shoulder and falls to the floor. The revolver slides across towards Frank. Everyone in the house dives to the floor in the darkness.

"We don't want anyone else hurt. Please drop your weapons and come out now or we will open fire." Smith announces over the speaker.

Frank looks up from the floor and sees the revolver. Billy, who is busy applying pressure to Adam's wound shouts at Kevin to kill the lights. Frank makes his move and slides the revolver underneath him.

Outside the house Smith is running around ordering halogens to be set up. The full beams from the police vans are hardly ideal for sharp shooters.

In the room Topher could see Frank's silhouette across the floor and watches as he fumbles about with something. As his eyes become accustomed to the dark Topher sees him slowly raising his arm and pointing it at Adam.

"Gun." Topher shouts as he dives forward to try and grab it. Before Topher reaches it Franks turns and fires a shot. Topher falls to the floor.

"Topher." Dylan shouts and dives across the floor to him. Outside one of the halogens is set up and is beamed through the living room window. Frank, still holding the revolver up, turns to face the window. A sharp shooter takes the shot and Frank's body crumbles to the floor.

Dylan cradles Topher as he lies in agony holding his stomach.

"I don't want to die Dylan."

"You're not going to die Topher."

"How bad is he?" Billy asks.

"He's loosing a lot of blood."

Billy crawls across the floor and tears opens Topher's top. He leans up and grabs a pillow from the sofa and takes the cover off. He placcs it on Topher's wound.

"Keep the pressure on this."

"Please put your weapons down and come out with your hands up." Smith pleads.

"Billy we have to get out of here." Kevin says.

"Okay. Guys make your way to the back door" He shouts as he crawls back over to Adam to help him. Dylan tries to move Topher but he is in too much pain.

"You'll have to leave him. It's okay. They'll take him to the hospital." Billy says.

"Dylan don't leave me." Topher says.

"Look. You can't come with us. You're bleeding really badly. There's an ambulance outside. They'll take care of you. You'll be okay Topher."

"Please Dylan. I don't want to go back to Borstal. I can't go back there."

"Come on Dylan." Casey says.

"Dylan please."

Dylan looks over at the guys as they crawl away and then back at Topher.

"You guys go. I'll stay here with Topher."

Adam stops crawling.

"Come on Adam. Keep going." Billy shouts.

"I'm staying too."

"What? Adam if you want to get out of here we've got to go now."

"We're in this together. If they don't go. I don't go." Billy turns around and looks at his friends.

"We'll go get him." They say.

They start to crawl back through the house when they hear a commotion from outside. A loud horn is sounding and people are shouting to get out of the way. Billy looks up to see a police van crashing through Frank's gates and straight through the front of the house. He lifts up his shotgun and points it at the driver.

"No don't shoot. It's Naz."

"Did you hear that Topher? It's Naz. He's came back for us. Come on, someone give me a hand." Dylan shouts as he tries to lift Topher.

They open the side door of the van and as everyone is getting in they can hear shots being fired from the other side. One of Billy's friends takes over the driving and reverses the van back out slowly. He keeps it in reverse. Billy who is also upfront in the van, fires a few blasts from the shotgun back at the policemen to make them take cover.

"Billy I need to get this thing turned around. Give them another target to shoot at."

"Like what?"

"Do you want me to spell it out?"

"Got you." Billy says as he clicks onto what he means.

"He takes his shotgun and hurries to the back of the van. He opens the door and fires a few rounds into the air making the police duck for cover again. This gives them a few seconds to turn the van. Billy looks at Kevin and they both grab hold of the grass. They throw him out into Frank's garden and as they go to shut the doors of the van behind them the grass points his revolver at Billy and fires. Billy and Kevin smile at him and close the doors.

"Right lets go." Billy shouts.

As the van turns the police take aim at the grass with his harmless weapon in his hand and open fire. The van takes off up the street as the police continue shooting at it.

"You came back for us. You came back." Casey says as he hugs Naz.

Naz smiles and hugs him back.

"How did you manage to drive the van?" Adam asks.

"I had a good teacher." Naz says looking at Topher.

"Come on Topher. Hang in there mate." Dylan says holding up his head.

The van rips along many side streets with a few patrol cars following them from a distance. The police know they will be fired upon if they appear too close. The van stops when it reaches a dead end.

"What do we do now?" Adam says.

"Don't worry. I, unlike you, thought this through." Billy says.

Dylan and Casey put each of Topher's arms over theirs and help him out of the van. They follow Billy's friends through a gap in the wall to two waiting cars.

Smith is informed of their escape and shouts at the officer, furiously demanding that he resign for being stupid enough to leave the keys in the police van. The officer pleads his case saying that it was when he was ordered to obtain the halogen lamps that they managed to steal the van.

"Do you know what? Don't resign. You're fired." He shouts at him as he walks away.

He sees his partner. "Twice, twice, they've left with our vehicles. How stupid can people be to leave keys in a police van while pursuing suspects?"

"Have we any leads as to where they are heading?" Smith calms down and thinks for a few seconds.

"We'll we know that one of them is seriously injured and he'll be needing medical attention so there's a slight possibility they'll drop him at the hospital depending on how bad it is. Also there was an escape route planned for Naz. I have the details. You drive while I radio in."

"What are you waiting on?"

"The keys."

Smith searches his pockets and then suddenly realises he has left them in the ignition.

"They're in the car." He mumbles.

Nevin looks at him and smirks. "Do you want me to inform the officer that you just fired not to hand in his badge just yet."

Smith puts his head down. Embarrassed, he climbs into the car.

22.

As they drove to their newly acquired hideout. Kevin stops the car he is driving and calls a doctor friend that he knows. He gives him the address and arranges for him to meet them there. The hideout was an old pool hall that was closed some time ago. It was only used now to store various stolen goods by Kevin's firm. As Adam lay on a table in a room out the back he was injected with a strong painkiller before the doc operated to remove the round from his shoulder. Billy appeared. He opened his pocket and took out
the letters.

"What's that?" Adam asks.

"The letters I sent. I eh…picked them up from you're friend Harry." says Billy

"Harry?…Linda and Harry?" Adam replies.
Billy smiles.

"How did you…?" asks Adam

"I went to see Kathy." Billy says.
Billy leaves him with the doc and he is patched up and ready to go in no time.
Topher was not so lucky. The doctor did what he could and left the room.

"So how is he?" Dylan asks.

"There's nothing I can do for him now. If he goes to hospital there is still only a fifty percent chance he will make it. He has lost so much blood and I don't have the equipment here to operate and remove the bullet."

Everyone's head goes down.

"Guys I've just called ahead and we have to be at Liverpool docks by early morning, we have a four hour journey ahead of us.
You have to make a decision. We can drop him near a hospital on the way." Billy says.

"I think we should let Topher decide." Dylan says.
Adam looks at Dylan and nods at the door to the other room. Dylan gets up and walks through. The rest of Billy's friends discuss their plans. Naz mentions his intended escape and how Smith had apparently set it up to let him go.

"Forget it. He wasn't letting you go anywhere." Kevin says.

"One thing, at least we know where Smith is right now." The door opens and Topher is on his feet with his arm around Dylan's shoulder helping himself up.

"Guys he's coming with us." Dylan says.
They all give Dylan a strange look.

"Its okay guys he knows he doesn't have long. But he wants to ride it out."

"Right, we had better move. I'll call ahead and make alternative arrangements for you Naz. There may be a few stops on the way but they'll get you there safely and you'll be well looked after."
Naz nods in acknowledgement before helping Dylan with Topher. The doctor gives Topher another injection.

"This will keep you numb for a while."
Topher smiles and all his friends smile back. But deep down they are only putting on a brave face as they know Topher won't last the night.

Two cars drive off from the hideout. The one in front contains two of Billy's friends and Naz with his new found friend, Casey. Kevin is driving the other car with Billy upfront. Adam is in the back with Dylan, Topher is in-between them. They reach the town centre and drive slowly along Riverside. As they approach the airport they can see many blue lights flashing. Topher is becoming weaker by the minute and is struggling to stay conscious.

"There's Smith's car." Billy says.

All the boys look out of the window at a flashy new car parked up on the pavement by the side of the road. Even Topher makes the effort to lift himself up to see it.

"Hey, how about you guys letting me go out with a bang." Topher says.

"What do you mean?" Dylan asks as he tries to hold back his tears.

"Come on. You know what I'm good at."

Adam and Dylan look at each other and nod.

"Billy, we need to make a stop." Adam says.

"Are you guys' crazy?" Billy pauses after saying this and thinks for a few seconds. He flashes the other car in front and both of them pull over. Billy leads the way back to the airport and they pull up about twenty metres from Smiths car. Dylan and Adam help Topher out of the car while Casey and Naz come running from the other one.

"What's going on?" Casey asks.

None of the boys answer. He looks at their long faces and realises what's happening.

"You have a scanner right." Topher says.

Billy holds it up and gets back into the car as he leaves the boys to say their goodbyes.

"Thanks for everything Dylan."

Dylan goes to say something but is choked up. The tears start to flow and he grabs Topher and puts his arms around him.

After Dylan releases him he turns around to see the rest of the boys crying.

"Hey come on guys, don't feel bad. We finished what we set out to do right?" says Topher.

"Topher we couldn't have done it without you. Jay would be proud." Dylan says with tears rolling down his cheeks. Topher puts his hand out with his palm facing down. Adam smiles and wipes his tears as he places his palm on top. Naz reaches forward and then Casey. Dylan looks on.

"Come on Dylan." Adam says.

Dylan smiles and slaps his hand down on top of the others.

"Right go. Get out of here. Oh and can you do me a favour guys?" asks Topher.

"What's that?" Dylan says.

"Don't get caught."

Billy tells his friend to go ride in the other car with Kevin so that all the boys can travel together with him. Adam gets in the front with Billy who has been waiting patiently and the other three get in the back. Topher watches as the two cars drive off out of sight as he struggles along the road towards Smith's car. His breathing is becoming more shallow with each step. There is a crowd gathered at the entrance to the airport with a heavy police presence. Reporters are running around setting up cameras hoping to obtain the first photo of the gang being captured. Topher reaches Smith's car and looks inside. The keys are dangling from the ignition. Topher smiles and then winces due to the pain. The injection the doctor gave him must be wearing off. He starts the engine and turns on the lights. The road up ahead is blocked so he reverses back a little and drives over a grass verge. Before he drives onto the main road he picks up the controls from the police radio.

"Hey Smith, I thought you would have learned by now,

not to leave your keys in your car." Topher says over the police airwaves.

Smith looks at his partner and starts running out of the airport.

"All cars, all cars, the gang are mobile in an unmarked patrol car. Headquarters can you do a trace?" Smith says as he reaches the main road to see the back of his car travelling back along the road towards Dundee. He runs to a patrol car and it's locked. He goes to the next one. It's locked. He shouts at an officer to hand him the keys to a car. By the time he gets on the road many other patrol cars have passed and are pursuing Topher.

"Good one Topher." Billy says as he sees the patrol cars speed past them in the opposite direction.
Topher looks in the mirror to see many lights flashing behind him. He turns on the stereo and flicks through Smith's tapes.

"Hey Smith you haven't got very good taste in music have you?" Topher says over the airwaves. He mentions a few of the titles much to Smith's embarrassment.

"It's okay, I've brought my own."
Topher takes a tape out of his pocket and slams it in the stereo. He keeps the control button down so that the music blasts out for everyone to hear. The boys smile at each other as they hear the rolling stones playing back to them through the scanner.

"You know where he's heading don't you?" Dylan says.

"Where?" Billy asks.

"The bridge."

"Come on Topher you can do it. Hang in there."
Casey shouts

Topher starts to sink further into the seat as he struggles to keep his eyes open. He puts his foot down on the accelerator and speeds up until he reaches the slip road onto the bridge. As he turns on the bend he picks up the controls to his mouth.

"Bye guys."

Topher holds the button down as he races towards the newly fitted barrier. He ducks down as he crashes through it. The control drops to the floor which cuts off the music from the airwaves and the boys sit patiently listening to the officers giving chase as they report back to Smith. The car hits the side of the bridge and flips up rolling over twice before eventually stopping after skidding along the road on its roof. Billy turns off the receiver.

"Way to go Topher." Adam mumbles.

The boys sit in silence for most of the journey. Billy thought they were asleep until he looked at them staring out the windows into the darkness. It was the early hours of the morning when Billy arrived at the docks. He is met by an acquaintance from the ship who directs them to an old security office. It is a small heated room with comfortable chairs and coffee making facilities. They are to stay here out of the way for a few hours until it is time to board. Billy's friends are to drive the two cars back to Dundee but decide to stay until the ship leaves. The next few hours go in quickly for the boys as they are entertained by listening to Billy's friends' story's about some of their past adventures in evading Smith. Naz is informed that he would be boarding a different ship and that it will be leaving soon. It's still dark when Adam, Dylan and Casey emerge from the office as they walk Naz out to say there goodbyes.

"You have the address of my brother's place right?" Adam says as he shakes his hand.

Naz nods and taps his pocket. He turns to Casey and offers

him his hand. Casey steps forward and unexpectedly grabs a hold of Naz with both hands and hugs him. Adam and Dylan look at each other in shock.

"Why don't you go with him Casey?" Dylan says.

"What? I can't go to India?"

"Why not? You would love it there, full of Pakis." Naz says laughing as he turns to shake Dylan's hand. Casey looks on embarrassed.

Naz is signalled to come on board.

"Guys please do as Topher asked. Don't get caught. I promise I'll write once I get settled."

Naz boards the ship and boys wave and go to walk away. Casey turns and makes a run for it and jumps on board the ship. Adam and Dylan turn and watch as he catches up with Naz. A few words are exchanged and Naz pats him on the shoulder. They turn and wave.

"I wish the rest of the guys could be here to see this." Adam says.

"What about Jay? What do think he would say?"

"I think he would be proud."

Adam and Dylan go back to the office and they all laugh when Adam explains about Casey. The laughter continues as Billy and his friends wind each other up as they reminisce over past times.

"I feel bad that I'm laughing. I feel like I should be grieving or something." Dylan says.

"It's a long boring boat ride. You'll have plenty of time to grieve later." Billy says as he overhears Dylan talking to Adam.

Adam can hardly keep his eyes open when they are informed that it is time to board. The sun is beginning to rise as they leave the office and the temperature has dropped considerably. Billy's friends are anxious to leave but walk with them. Adam and Dylan look on at their unemotional goodbye, as if they'll see each other in the pub the next day. They board the ship and Dylan mentions that he keeps expecting Smith to turn up any minute and stop them. They watch from the edge as it drifts slowly away from the dock. After making the final payment for their travel, Billy finds the boys and shows them to their accommodation. It is a tiny room with bunk beds and Billy informs them that he is in the room next door if they need anything. Adam steps in and checks out the beds. He looks down at the lower bunk then quickly jumps up to claim the top one as this one has the porthole view. He lies back and watches as the dock appears further and further away.

"Hey Adam. Do you think Casey will be alright with Naz."

Adam laughs at the thought of Casey being in an Asian country with his racist attitude.

"He'll be fine. And anyway according to Naz the Pakis will look after him."

They both laugh and nothing more is said between them as they drift off to sleep with a happy thought.

~

23.

One year later

Adam awakens with the hot sun shinning on his face through the gap in the curtain. Billy usually has to drag him out of bed for work in the morning, but not today. He's up before anyone else and heads straight for the kitchen to pour himself some cereal. He sits out on the balcony and munches away as he watches the large boats enter and leave the harbour down below. Adam savours every moment of this relaxing time as he knows it won't be long before he is out in the hot baking sun, sanding and painting some of the smaller boats nearer the shore. Although he turned sixteen recently and is old enough to leave and travel on his own he likes it here and for the first time in a long time he feels happy and settled. His thoughts start to drift back to his past and the many different homes he encountered whilst growing up. Each new surrounding bringing something different into his life. It isn't long after these thoughts enter his head that they soon disappear as he is distracted by a noise in the kitchen. He knows it can't be Dylan, as he's worst at getting up in the morning.

"Oh you're up. I was just about to wake you" Billy says as he pours himself some coffee and joins Adam on the balcony.

"Why are you up so early?"

"I don't know, I just woke up." Adam says in between slurps of milk and cereal.

"Well you'll be happy to hear that you'll only be working a half day today."

"Why is that?"

"I have to go and pick up some supplies."

"I thought they delivered them?"

"I need them now and I could wait days on them being delivered so it'll be quicker to drive through and pick them up, also Nina wants to go shopping."

Although this is the main holiday resort on the island and contains the most bars and restaurants there are no hardware stores. The nearest is a long drive to the other side of the island. Adam smiles at the thought of having the afternoon off and lounging around on the beach.

"You and Dylan could come with us if you want."

"Nah, I think I'll just stay here, Dylan might want to go with you though," Adam says sarcastically.

He finishes his cereal and wakens Dylan with the good news. Adam has never seen Dylan move so quickly to get up for work.

They arrive at the boat shed, which is situated not far from the beach. As Billy goes into the office and makes himself more coffee, Adam and Dylan open the large wooden doors and pull out the trailer containing the boat they've been working on over the past few days. It's a small sanding job but it's been hard work for them with the amount of layers of paint that have been applied in the past. Billy could have left the boys working on it while he was away for the day but he knows they deserve time off. Ever since they arrived on the island Billy has had them working nearly every day from early till late. Adam is not stupid though and knows what Billy is doing. He's keeping them busy so that they are too tired to get themselves into trouble. When they do have a day off it usually results in

Billy taking them on a pub-crawl where they get to mingle with the holiday-makers. Dylan, although he acts a bit slow sometimes is certainly not slow when it comes to girls, he's always the first one over chatting to them. Billy just sits back and leaves them to it. He pays their wages to them in cash and if they choose to spend it on some girl in one night then that's up to them. He was like that once himself and knows how they think.

The boat the boys have been working on looks like a small toy next to some of the larger boats around by the harbour. They wheel the trailer out as far as the extension line will go so that they can work on the boat while out in the sun. The boys prefer jobs like this as they can watch what's going on around them as they work. Later in the morning when the beach starts to fill up they usually end up with a few admirers who come over for a chat and watch them at work. With all the attention they had not long ago, it's quite surprising that nobody has ever recognised them. Adam has grown his hair long since then and according to Dylan he looks more like a hippie surfer than a dangerous violent murderer that the papers described him as. Dylan hasn't changed though; he still looks the same as that first day when Adam was introduced to him. Tall, dopey looking and scars from head to toe. Adam also has many scars but his are more of the psychological kind. The ones that feel engraved into his memory that no one can see. The one's that nearly sent him over the edge and that he tries his hardest to forget. For a long time he blamed Billy for everything that happened to him, but how was he to know what would happen.

Since they arrived on the island Billy has talked about what happened and explained to Adam that he was not much older than he is now when it all started. He had got himself into so much trouble he had no option but to leave or face doing some serious jail time. Billy had gone to see him before he left and made sure Old Charlie and Kathy were taking care of him. He thought he would have been okay. It wasn't Billy's fault, it was the authorities, they knew what was going on, but did nothing.

Nina arrives with the sandwiches and cold juice for everyone and they all sit in the shade as they enjoy the break from the hot sun.

"So what are you guys going to do today?" Billy asks.

"Probably just go to the beach and chill out" Adam says as he looks at Dylan and they both nod at each other.

"Yeah, well make sure you don't do anything stupid and get yourself into any trouble.

"Why do you always say that? We haven't been in trouble since we got here...well except from that time when that man came looking for me because Dylan got his daughter drunk" Adam says.

"That was funny," Dylan says.

"Maybe for you, but you weren't the one who had some crazy man running after you accusing you of all sorts."

"Look guys, I just don't want to come back and have the police at me. The next thing everyone will know who you are," Billy says, looking concerned.

Adam thinks about this for a second and realises what Billy is taking about, the slightest hint of the wrong people knowing where he was, would escalate to the place swarming with British reporters all trying to get a photo of him and Dylan. He has left that life behind him but it could all come back with one stupid mistake.

They finish their sandwiches and get back to work. The rest of the morning goes in quickly for the boys and before they know it Billy has started putting the tools back into the shed. Adam stops to look out onto the beach as it's already starting to get crowded with holidaymakers soaking up the rays from the sun. Billy nudges Dylan and makes a comment that he is eyeing up some ugly fat girl.

"I think she's alright," Dylan says, also stopping to look at her. Adam looks at Billy and they all laugh.

"No need to guess what you two will be doing all day," Billy says.

After locking up the boat shed Nina drives the boy's back to the apartment.

"We'll be back about six" Billy says as they drive off. The boys go up to the apartment to get changed and are back out within minutes holding towels under their arms. As they walk down the road to the beach they pass a small shop and decide to buy some ice cream. Adam also picks up a newspaper.

"Twentieth of the ninth, ninety. Not bad, only a day old" Adam says as Dylan raises his eyebrows. Adam likes to catch up on what's happening back in Britain even though the papers are sometimes a day or two late. Dylan refuses to read them after all the lies they printed about them. Adam didn't mind, in a way he kind of liked all the attention, even though sometimes the stories were wrong and quite hurtful.

They make their way to their favourite place on the beach. A small sandy platform, where from this position, even when lying down they can view the whole beach and in there minds…girls?

"Why do you bother buying those?" Dylan says as Adam opens the newspaper.

"I just like to find out what's been going on back home"

"What? You don't consider this home?"

"Yeah of course, I mean…ah you know what I mean."

"Do you ever think about going back?"

"Sometimes. But I know it would only be to cause more trouble."

"Yeah me too, I still think about Sarah. I sometimes wonder what she's doing right now and if she ever thinks about me."

"Of course she does"

"You think so?"

"I'm quite sure."

"I was about to call her a while back."

"Did you?"

"No. it would have been pointless really." He says looking away.

"You did. Didn't you?"

Dylan looks back with a cheeky grin.

"So what did she say?"

"She just asked how I was and stuff."

"Do you ever think about going back to see her?"

"Yeah, all the time. Not like just to see her but if I was ever back for another reason I think it would be good to look her up to see how she was."

"I hope you didn't mention where we were."

"Come on Adam I may look stupid."

"Yeah. You do look stupid."

Dylan dives on Adam and they both wrestle for a few seconds.

"Dylan I don't get you mate. When any girls are around you are the first one over trying to chat them up but here you are mopping about some girl you haven't seen in over a year"

"I know but she was different, kind of special."

Adam gives Dylan a funny look and he is about to jump on him and wrestle again when some other random girl in a bikini walks past and distracts him. She smiles at them before walking into the sea.

"I'll be back in a minute." Dylan says as he gets up to go and speak to her.

"See what I mean" Adam says as he picks up the newspaper and turns on his side so that he can read it. He opens it up and smiles as he sees an old photo of himself staring back at him. The story that accompanies the photo is another update of the on going inquiry into the death of Jay. *'An ex Dundee Councillor has been charged with conspiracy to murder.'* They never show a photo of the councillor but it does give them an excuse to print a whole page about Adam and his so called gang. The story has been reprinted time and time again over the past year. Each time there is a new development no matter how trivial, they make it a double page spread and add more lies to it. That's the reason Dylan refuses to read them as he gets himself worked up when someone that he has never even met before has something to say about it.

The story goes on to say that the Councillor paid the two wardens who worked on the program extra bonuses to disrupt the boy's rehabilitation.

'It is now believed that the two wardens were tragically killed in circumstances related to the boys' quest for retribution for the killing of their Program's leader Jason Fallon.'

Adam looks at the photo of Jay and then reads on.

'A third warden who is believed to have been murdered by his two now deceased workmates is the brother of Heather Low. The ex-councillor's assistant. She is apparently the key witness against the ex-councillor and will produce evidence to prove that he paid the two wardens to sabotage the Program. She will also produce a notebook containing

complaints that Fallon had recorded each time the wardens attacked the boys.

Adam has read most of this before and looks down the page to another paragraph accompanied with the story. *'In a separate case against the ex-councillor a local businessman Tony Walker, father of Casey Walker, one of the gang who is still at large, was giving evidence against Williamson who apparently handed contracts illegally to his company for favours.'* Adam looks at the photo of Casey and smiles. Nobody will ever find him. The last letter Adam and Dylan had from Naz was to say that Casey was now in a relationship with a young girl. An Indian girl. There is also a small photo of Smith, who after the boys' escape was investigated and forced into early retirement. This was due to his obsession with the case and for allowing the boys to run free in an effort to track down another criminal from his past. He will also be called upon to give evidence in the up and coming trial of the ex-councillor.

"We never had a chance" Adam mumbles to himself as he closes the newspaper and throws it aside. He now wishes he had taken Dylan's advice and not read it. He turns to lie on his stomach and catches sight of Dylan splashing around in the water with the bikini girl. He closes his eyes and smiles as his mind drifts off and he thinks about the first time that he met Dylan. The same day he met Jay and the rest of the boys on the program.

The End